"Why are you help[ing me]? Do you expect something from me in return?

I don't have a lot of money with me, but—"

He grabbed her hand. "I don't need your money. What do you think I am?"

"I'm sorry. I didn't mean to insult you."

He tried not to look at her, but the feel of her fingers, soft on his skin, drew him in. Her gaze was full of remorse.

"You've been good to me. I don't know how to thank you."

"You already did."

"Well, thanks again for everything," she said as they reached her hotel. Then she let go of his hand, turned and walked away.

He tamped down the urge to follow her inside, but didn't leave. He'd be there, hiding, waiting.

Staying by her side, day and night, would be his priority for as long as someone still wanted her dead.

PAULA GRAVES

FORBIDDEN TOUCH

HARLEQUIN®

TORONTO • NEW YORK • LONDON
AMSTERDAM • PARIS • SYDNEY • HAMBURG
STOCKHOLM • ATHENS • TOKYO • MILAN • MADRID
PRAGUE • WARSAW • BUDAPEST • AUCKLAND

For Gayle Wilson, whose wonderful stories made me
want to be a Harlequin Intrigue author in the first place.

ISBN-13: 978-0-373-69313-9
ISBN-10:   0-373-69313-3

FORBIDDEN TOUCH

Copyright © 2008 by Paula Graves

ABOUT THE AUTHOR

Alabama native Paula Graves wrote her first book, a mystery starring herself and her neighborhood friends, at age six. A voracious reader, Paula loves books that pair tantalizing mystery with compelling romance. When she's not reading or writing, she works as a creative director for a Birmingham advertising agency and spends time with her family and friends. She is a member of Southern Magic Romance Writers, Heart of Dixie Romance Writers and Romance Writers of America.

Paula invites readers to visit her Web site, www.paulagraves.com.

Books by Paula Graves

HARLEQUIN INTRIGUE
926—FORBIDDEN TERRITORY
998—FORBIDDEN TEMPTATION
1046—FORBIDDEN TOUCH

CAST OF CHARACTERS

Iris Browning—Her empathic abilities warn her of Mariposa island's dark underbelly. Will her quest to find her missing friend put her own life in jeopardy?

Maddox Heller—The former government agent wonders why a CIA operative is so interested in Iris. Is she connected to the terrorists whose deadly embassy siege cost him his career?

Sandrine Beck—She invited Iris to join her for a week in the sun. Now she's missing. Is her disappearance connected to the other strange things happening on Mariposa?

Alexander Quinn—Who is this mysterious man following Iris all over the island?

Boris Grinkov—The former Russian scientist is the head of the Cassandra Society, a secretive organization dedicated to the scientific measurement of psychic phenomena.

Tahir Mahmoud—The young Kaziristani businessman is charming and urbane—but not without secrets.

Celia Shore—The famous psychic to the stars shows up bleeding on a deserted beach, with no memory of coming to Mariposa. Do her lost memories hold the key to finding Sandrine?

Nicholas Darcy—The Regional Security Officer at the American Consulate in Mariposa knows Maddox by reputation. Should he believe the disgraced agent's fears about the danger to Iris Browning?

Chapter One

Pain snaked up Iris Browning's spine and squeezed, stealing her breath. She stumbled to a halt, her sudden stop earning a French epithet from a blonde walking on the sidewalk behind her. The woman swung her head around as she passed, glaring and gesturing.

"Sorry," Iris murmured, moving off the sun-baked sidewalk and leaning against the warm stucco facade of a dive shop. She breathed deeply, the tangy sea air filling her lungs and beginning to clear her pain-fuzzed brain.

"Are you okay, sugar?" A man's drawl, molasses-slow and unmistakably Southern, rumbled from somewhere to her right. She opened her eyes, squinting against the tropical sun, and found a pair of slate-blue eyes fixed on her.

The speaker was not a local, though his sun-bronzed skin suggested he'd been in the tropics awhile. He sat at a small wooden table near the front of an open-air café. His long, muscular legs stretched out in front of him, clad in a pair of denim cutoffs that had seen better days. His cotton T-shirt, though worn loose and untucked, did little to hide his broad shoulders or muscular chest.

Iris raised her eyes to meet his curious gaze. "I'm fine."

He pushed back from the table, his chair scraping the concrete floor, and stood to face her. "You don't look fine."

"Gee, thanks." She tried for sardonic but didn't quite achieve it. Annoyed at her weakness, she pushed away from the wall. Her knees wobbled but she managed to stay upright.

Remember why you're here, Iris.

Ignoring her instinct to run, she crossed to him and pulled a photo from her pocket. It was becoming dog-eared, thanks to her morning's efforts. "Have you seen this woman?"

The stranger's brow wrinkled as he studied the face. "Can't say I have." He looked up. "Friend of yours?"

"She was supposed to meet me yesterday afternoon. She didn't show." The anxiety writhing in her stomach had been building since she'd arrived by cab at the hotel to discover Sandrine missing. The concierge had told her Sandrine hadn't checked out, but none of her friend's things were in the room she and Iris were supposed to share. Iris didn't want to think the worst, but the alternatives didn't make much sense.

As the blue-eyed stranger handed the photo back to her, his fingers brushed hers. A dark sensation roiled through her, pulling her attention back to the present. It wasn't physical pain, like the earlier sensation, but an emotional one, black and bitter like strong coffee.

She jerked her hand back, losing her grip on the photo. It fluttered to the floor, faceup.

The man's eyes narrowed as he picked up the photo and handed it to her. "Sorry. Didn't mean to invade your personal space."

She realized how he must have interpreted her quick retreat from his touch. "You didn't," she assured him, her voice more gruff than she intended. The blackness swirling through her thickened, slowed to a poisonous crawl.

"You're not used to this heat. Why don't you sit down? I'll buy you something to drink."

She looked up at him, intending to refuse. But the wariness in his eyes struck a nerve. Her earlier reaction to his touch had wounded him, somehow. She found herself unable to compound the insult by rebuffing his offer.

Besides, she was tired and thirsty.

Relenting, she sat in the chair he held out for her. The stranger disappeared for a moment, returning with a chilled bottle of water, already uncapped. He set it in front of her and took the chair on the opposite side of the table.

"Name's Maddox." His gaze followed the bottle to her lips.

Iris began to take a sip, then stopped. How many rules of traveling alone had she just broken? She set the bottle back on the table and looked nervously at her companion.

A wry smile curved his lips, carving dimples in his bronzed cheeks. She felt a bubble of unexpected attraction pop and spread through her chest. "Sorry. Guess I should have left it unopened. I'll get you another one."

She shook her head. "I'm okay." She started to stand, but fresh pain assaulted her, driving her back to her seat.

"I'll get you another one," he repeated firmly.

She watched him cross to the bar and order another water. He paid in cash and brought the unopened bottle back to her. She opened the bottle and took a sip.

"Had any sleep?" he asked.

She eyed him warily. "How bad do I look?"

Maddox grabbed the other bottle of water and took a swig before he spoke. "You look tired. A little pale. Not bad."

"I just want to find Sandrine."

"That's a pretty name." He gestured at the photo on the table. "Pretty girl. Maybe she met somebody here—"

Iris shook her head. "She'd have left a message."

He leaned toward her, flashing a grin just this side of naughty. "Love makes you forget your own name, sugar."

"She would have left a message," she repeated firmly, forcing her gaze away from those dimples.

"Give her time. Maybe she will." He sat back again, slouching low in his seat. One sandy lock of hair flopped into his eyes; he shook it away from his face and leveled his gaze with hers. "You have somewhere to stay, don't you?"

She nodded quickly. "She'd already checked in for us."

"Well, that's good." His voice softened, almost as if he were speaking to a child. "Maybe you should head on back to your room until later in the day. The sun down here in the islands isn't like what you're used to in the States."

"I live in Alabama. I know about heat." She immediately felt foolish for giving him even that much personal information.

"I'm from Georgia, myself," he said, a smile in his voice. "Bet you couldn't tell, huh? Been working on losing my accent."

She couldn't hold back a soft chuckle.

He smiled at her, flashing that dimple again. It had a similar effect, twisting her stomach into a knot. "That's better. Laughter's the best medicine, they say."

"I'm Iris." She managed a tight smile.

"Nice to meet you, Iris. That's another pretty name."

She ignored the compliment. "Are you here on vacation?"

"No, ma'am, I live here year-round."

"Because Georgia just wasn't hot enough for you?"

"In the summer Georgia's hotter than here." He slumped deeper in the tiny café chair. "It's nice year-round here in Mariposa. Never so hot that a sea breeze can't perk you up and never so cool that you need to wear socks with your flip-flops."

"How does one support oneself on a tropical island?" she asked, giving in to a twinge of curiosity.

"One lives off one's trust fund, sugar." He laughed. "Or odd jobs. Whichever is available."

"What odd jobs do you do?"

"Don't think I look like the trust fund type?"

She flushed, embarrassed by her assumption. "I'm sorry—"

"I do security work. Here and there."

Mysterious, she thought, her wariness returning. She'd grown too relaxed over the past few minutes. Not smart, dropping her guard all alone in a strange place.

"Have you talked to the police about your friend?" Maddox asked after another long swig of water.

The question disarmed her a bit. "They didn't seem terribly concerned. They said she's a grown-up, it hasn't even been twenty-four hours yet—"

"Blah blah blah," he finished with a sympathetic nod. "How about family and other friends? Did you check with them?"

"She doesn't have a family, and I don't know that much about her life or who her other friends are." She could tell her answer confused him, so she continued. "Sandrine is a friend from college. We live in different states now. We do talk on the phone now and then, but I don't know much about her life and she doesn't know about mine. That's part of what this weekend was going to be about—catching up."

"Well, maybe it still will be," Maddox said. "In fact, I bet when you get back to the hotel, your friend'll be waitin' for you with some crazy story about how she got waylaid."

Iris wished she could believe him. But the sense of unease that had hit her the second she stepped from the plane in Sebastian had grown to full-blown foreboding, as palpable as the pain still pulsing up and down her spine.

"You don't buy that, do you?" Maddox murmured.

"Sandrine's levelheaded. She wouldn't go off with someone she'd just met, and she wouldn't have blown off meeting me at the airport when she worked so hard to talk me into this trip." Iris looked down at Sandrine's face in the photo, the ever-present smile and the sparkle of mischief in her green eyes. "And then I think about that missing girl over in—"

"Don't go there yet." Maddox reached across the table and brushed the back of her hand with his fingertips. Once again she experienced a strange, dark sensation spiral up her arm from the point of contact. The emotion it evoked inside her remained frustratingly nebulous—dark, painful but undefined.

She forced herself not to pull her hand away this time.

"How about the U.S. consulate?" he asked, sliding his hand away. "Have you checked with anybody there?"

"They suggested I call the police." She picked up Sandrine's photo and put it in the front pocket of her purse. "What do I owe you for the water, Mr. Maddox?"

"Just Maddox. No mister. And the water's on me."

"Thank you." When she stood, he stood with her, the polite gesture at odds with his scruffy appearance.

"I hope you find your friend." He sounded sincere. "Tell you what—when she turns up, bring her down here and I'll buy you both a drink. Just ask for Mad Dog. Everybody knows me."

She inclined her head toward him and headed out of the café. The sun slammed into her head like a ninety-degree sledgehammer, sapping her remaining energy as she trudged toward the beach, where the Hotel St. George hovered like a pale pink jewel over the cobalt-blue waters of Cutler's Bay.

The closer she got to the beach, the stronger the smell of the sea, sharp and salty in the breeze that lifted her hair and dried the perspiration beading on her forehead and arms. But mingled with the sea air, an undercurrent of misery lingered. It weighted on Iris as she neared the palm-studded beach stretching for a mile around the bay.

Someone was out there. Someone in agony. Physical pain, sharp and specific, etched phantom slashes along the skin of Iris's wrists and ankles. A throbbing pain bloomed in the back of her skull, blinding in its intensity.

Her vision blurred, the world around her beginning to spin out of control. She groped for something to hold on to, something to keep her from pitching forward into the street, but there was nothing. Nothing but the blare of car horns and a muted cacophony of voices.

And pain. Knee-buckling, back-bending pain.

She crumpled to her knees, the sting of the rough pavement on her bare flesh little more than a twinge against the onslaught of agony racing circles around her nervous system.

She tried to lift her head, tried to regain her bearings, but nothing around her looked real or recognizable. It was as if the pain itself had become tangible, a red mist surrounding her, blinding her to everything else around her.

In the heart of that mist, a man's voice called her name.

MADDOX HELLER kept his distance behind the pale wraith of a woman who'd interrupted his morning, trying not to think too long or hard about why he was venturing out into the mid-morning heat to follow a tourist to her hotel. Sure, she was pretty enough—or would be if she didn't look like death walking—but Mariposa was full of pretty women, more than a few of whom wouldn't kick him out of bed for snoring. So why was he so interested in Iris the Jet-lagged Tourist and her woeful little tale?

Hell, Mad Dog, maybe you're just bored.

Two years in paradise might seem like heaven to some folks, but there was only so much sunshine and sea air a man could take before he needed something different to occupy his thoughts.

After Kaziristan—

He stopped short. No revisiting Kaziristan. That was rule number one of Maddox's new life. He'd wasted a year wallowing in what-ifs after Kaziristan. Damn near drove him insane.

A block ahead, Iris the Jet-lagged Tourist suddenly pitched forward, hitting the pavement hard, knees first. Maddox's heart lurched into double time and he sprinted toward her, splitting his attention between Iris and the crowd around her. Like any tourist mecca, Mariposa had its share of thieves and pickpockets. A likely suspect was already lurking, a wiry boy in his late teens on a bicycle.

"Iris!" he called, closing the distance between them.

He saw Iris groping on the ground as if blind. She found her purse and snatched it up, hugging it tight to her chest, turning her head toward his voice.

He pushed through the small crowd of people gathering around her and crouched by her side. "Iris?"

Her head jerked up, her gaze sliding toward him without quite meeting his. He touched her arm and she jumped like a frightened animal, jerking her arm away from him.

"It's Maddox. From the café, remember?" He took her hand, holding on when she started to pull away. "You fell."

Her eyes focused on his face, her pupils dilated. Perspiration sparkled on her forehead. "I'm okay."

"No, you're not. Let me call an ambulance."

She released his hand. "I just need to get to my hotel."

Maddox bit back further protest, glancing at the gathered crowd around him. "Then let me help you do that, at least." He held out his hand to her one more time.

She looked around her, color creeping up her throat and settling in the center of her pale cheeks. She let him help her up, her body swaying toward his. She smelled of heat and honeysuckle, taking him to a time and place he hadn't revisited in years. Twin phantoms of loss and longing danced in his head.

Iris gasped softly, her steps faltering. She tugged her hand away, her face lifting to his. "It's too much."

He stared at her, not following.

A neutral mask settled over her face. She squared her shoulders and started walking forward at a faster pace.

It lasted only a few feet before she stumbled again. Maddox caught her up as she started to fall.

"Someone's hurt," Iris whispered.

Maddox frowned, even more confused. "Who's hurt?"

"Help! Somebody call 911!" A woman's voice, high and frantic, drew his attention. He spotted a woman in a bathing suit waving her arms as she jogged awkwardly up the beach.

The woman in the bathing suit caught sight of Maddox and Iris. "There's a woman on the beach. She's injured." The woman staggered to a stop and tried to catch her breath.

Maddox looked down at Iris, the hair on his arms rising. Her coffee-brown eyes met his briefly before she dropped her gaze and lowered her chin almost to her chest.

He grabbed his cell phone from his pocket and gave a terse report when the emergency operator answered. By now, several people had responded to the woman's cries for help. Tourists and locals alike followed as she jogged back down the beach out of sight. Iris lifted her head and started walking toward the beach, obviously intent on following.

"Where do you think you're going?" Maddox caught up with her. "You can barely stand."

"I can help her—"

He grabbed her elbow. "I've called for help. They'll be here in a couple of minutes. You need to get out of the sun and get some bandages on those cuts." He gestured at her legs.

Her gaze dropped to where blood from her injured knees ran down her shins in slow rivulets. Her brow wrinkled as if she hadn't realized she was hurt. "They're just scrapes."

"Scrapes can get infected if they're not cleaned."

Her expression tightened. "I know what I'm doing." She pulled away and headed for the wooden steps leading from the street to the beach, leaving him little option but to follow her or walk away.

Every instinct he had screamed at him to walk away.

But his legs chose to follow.

Maybe it was adrenaline or sheer female stubbornness, but Iris seemed to find a second wind, moving through the sand with long, steady strides. Maddox caught up with her, sidling a glance at her. She still looked pale, dark circles under her eyes and lines of weariness etched in her forehead, but she didn't falter as she reached the circle of onlookers ringing a woman lying near the water's edge.

"I need to get to her," she murmured, looking up at Maddox.

He narrowed his eyes. "Are you a doctor or something?"

"Just get me to her," she said more firmly.

He edged through the crowd, bringing Iris with him. While she crouched by the woman, taking her hand, Maddox made a quick visual assessment of the woman's injuries. Definitely not a local; her tan was the chemical variety, and not even the crusted sand and seawater could hide the fact that her crumpled linen suit was designer quality. Her feet were bare, with angry red ligature welts circling both narrow ankles. Similar marks marred her slender wrists.

Her face was pale beneath the tan, smeared vestiges of makeup faintly visible around her eyes and lips. Though her eyes were closed, she was making low moaning sounds, confirming that she was at least partially conscious.

The woman who'd called for help sat by the injured woman's head, gently stroking matted hair away from her face. "Did anyone call paramedics?" she asked.

"They're on the way," Maddox assured her. Since it looked as if Iris was going to do nothing but hold the injured woman's hand, he knelt and checked the woman's pulse. Slow but strong. That was a good sign. But her skin was cool to the touch, suggesting she might be slipping toward shock. "Does anyone have a beach towel or something we can use to cover her?"

A man from the crowd offered a multicolored beach blanket. Maddox dusted off the loose sand and folded it over the woman.

She gave a swift gasp, her eyes snapping open to meet Iris's gaze. The sudden movement caught Maddox by surprise, sending him rocking onto his backside in the soft sand.

A groan rumbled from Iris's throat and she let go of the woman's hand. Her face glistened with perspiration and deeper shadows bruised the delicate flesh around her eyes. Trying to rise from her crouch, she ended up on her rear in the sand.

She lifted her eyes to Maddox. "She has a concussion.

The back of her head. I don't think she has any other serious injuries." Her voice was thin. Breathless.

He forced his attention back to the injured woman, who was trying to sit up. Maddox gently held her still. "The medics'll be here any minute, darlin'. Hear the sirens? Just lie still."

Her blue eyes locked with his. "I don't remember...."

He patted her shoulder. "You may have a bump on your head." He glanced at Iris. She was staring at the woman.

The sound of sirens died. In seconds, two Sebastian paramedics pushed through the crowd to flank the victim.

Maddox moved out of their way, heading for Iris's side. She struggled to her feet, ignoring the hand he offered to help her up, and turned her gaze toward the pink facade of Hotel St. George a hundred yards down the beach. Her shoulders slumped.

"Just a few yards," Maddox coaxed, wrapping his arm around her waist. Her body vibrated like a tuning fork where he touched her. He tightened his hold on her, and half carried her down the beach toward the hotel. As they neared the back entrance, her stumbling gait faltered, her legs giving out.

Maddox lifted her into his arms. She was lighter than she looked, her loose cotton dress hiding the fact that she was almost painfully thin. She made a soft sound of protest that he ignored, then settled her head against his shoulder, her breath shallow and rapid against his throat.

He carried her to one of the cedar benches flanking the walkway. She slumped in the corner of the bench and looked up at him, her gaze unfocused.

He crouched beside her, his heart pounding more from concern than exertion. "Iris? Do you have your room key?"

She struggled to sit up, reaching for her handbag. Suddenly, she pitched forward, her forehead slamming into his mouth. Pain rocketed through his lip, eliciting a soft curse as he caught her to keep her from toppling to the concrete walk.

"Iris?" He eased her head back, brushing her hair away from her face. Her eyes were closed. Her head was a dead weight in his hand.

She was unconscious.

Chapter Two

"Welcome back."

Iris blinked, her vision slowly clearing. Over her head, rattan ceiling fan blades slowly circled, stirring the air around her. The light was off, but muted sunlight filtering through the curtains cast a saffron glow over the white walls.

She was in her hotel room. In her bed.

And sitting next to her, his elbows propped on his knees, was the sandy-haired stranger she'd met at the open-air café.

She bolted upright, scooting back toward the wicker headboard of the hotel bed. "What are you doing here?"

He sat back, his expression shuttering. "Just sittin' here wonderin' if you were ever going to wake up. I was about to call a doctor."

Memory seeped into her foggy brain. The woman at the beach. Her missing friend. "Sandrine," she murmured.

"Sorry, sugar. She's still not here."

She leaned back. "How long was I asleep?"

Maddox lifted one dark eyebrow. "You weren't sleepin'. You were out for the count."

"How long?" she repeated, fear blooming in her chest. It was getting worse. Discomfort had always been part of her gift, but in recent years, the intensity of pain had increased, her recovery periods extending from minutes to hours to days.

"About ten minutes. I got your room key out of your purse. Hope you don't mind." Maddox handed her the slim card key. "You got a first aid kit around here? We should check your temperature, make sure you're not hyperthermic."

Hyperthermic? She slanted a look at him, surprised he'd use such a fancy word for sunstroke. He didn't look the type. "I'm not overheated," she said.

"You sure?" He pressed the back of his hand to her forehead, frowning. "You still look awfully pale. Maybe I should call that doctor after all."

Iris shook her head. "There's nothing a doctor can do."

He stared at her, his expression queasy as he apparently jumped to the wrong conclusion. "Oh, God. I'm sorry."

"No—no. It's not fatal," she assured him quickly.

Just crippling, she added silently.

"Glad to hear it." A smile dimpled his cheeks, but his gaze remained wary, and she could feel him retreating from her.

She quelled a sense of disappointment and tucked the bedcovers more snugly around her. "I'm okay now. Really," she added, not missing the skepticism in his expression. "I'm going to rest a little and get something to eat."

"Then what?"

"Then I guess I'll call the police again and see if I can get them interested in Sandrine's disappearance."

He nodded slowly, watching her through narrowed

eyes. For the first time, she noticed his lower lip looked red and puffy.

"What happened to your lip?" she asked when it became clear he wasn't going to say anything else.

"You're a hardheaded woman."

That explained the pain in her forehead. "I'm so sorry."

He shrugged off her apology. "No worries, sugar. The bleeding didn't even last that long."

"You don't have to babysit me. I'm all right now."

"At the beach—do you remember—?" He paused and started again. "You told me someone was hurt. And then a few seconds later, a woman ran up the beach calling for help because another woman was hurt. How did you know?"

The answer would only lead to more questions she didn't want to answer. Not now. Not to a stranger. "I guess I heard the woman calling before you did."

He pressed his lips together but didn't ask anything else. He stood up, towering over her bedside. The light from outside cast him in shadow, hiding all but outlines of his strong, square features. He touched her shoulder. "It was interesting meetin' you, Iris. I hope you find your friend."

Fire licked her skin where his fingers lay, spreading heat over her collarbone and into her chest. Pain, thick and black, trembled under the surface of his touch, a reminder of the sensation she'd felt when Maddox first touched her at the café. He was as much in pain as the woman at the beach, though his pain came from somewhere inside him.

If she were stronger, she might risk what she called a

drawing, a deliberate attempt to ease the distress she could feel festering inside him. But whatever was eating at him was big and strong and old. She didn't know if she could bear it.

"The offer stands. You find your friend, bring her to town and I'll buy you both a drink."

"Thank you," she repeated, almost sagging with relief when he removed his hand from her shoulder and walked to the door. The tightness in her chest receded, the blackness ebbing from the edges of her vision.

He turned in the open doorway, his head slanting as he gazed back at her. "If the police don't help you, let me know."

"What can you do?"

He smiled. "I know people who know people."

"Are any of those people private detectives?"

His only answer was a widening of his smile as he closed the door behind him.

"MAN COME lookin' for you, Mad Dog." Claudell Savoy looked up from behind the bar when Maddox entered the Beachcomber, a tiny hole-in-the-wall dive that catered more to locals than the tourist crowd. "Seem real interested in where you at."

Maddox shot the grizzled Creole bartender a wary look. "You tell him anything?"

"Not me, man." Claudell didn't sound convincing.

"For enough cash, you'd sell out your mama. What'd you tell him?" Maddox slid onto a bar stool in front of Claudell. He was the only one around; the bar wouldn't open for another hour, but Claudell never minded the company.

"I jus' say I see you around here sometime." Claudell

grinned, looking proud of himself. "He give me twenty dollars."

Maddox frowned. "Thanks, buddy."

"You ain't nobody's buddy, man. We both know that." Claudell set a tumbler in front of him and pulled out a bottle of rye whiskey. "Here. On the house."

Maddox put his hand over the glass. "Rain check." The temptation to drown his chronic dissatisfaction in liquor was getting a little too strong these days.

Claudell shrugged and put the glass back in a rack behind the bar. "Say, I remember somethin' else 'bout that man."

Maddox met the bartender's expectant gaze. "I ain't givin' you twenty bucks, Claudell. Good try, though."

Claudell shrugged, smiling. "Bah, I tell you for nothin'. He say someone name Celia lookin' for you."

"I don't know any Celia."

"He say she wanna talk to you. Real important."

He didn't like the sound of that. "What'd he look like?"

Claudell grimaced. "You know. Tourist."

Great, that narrowed it down. "Did he say where I could find him if I happened to want to talk to this Celia?"

"Didn't say. Give me this, though." Claudell reached into the chest pocket of his stained white uniform shirt and retrieved a business card.

Maddox took it from him. "Charles Kipler Management," he read aloud. An address in Beverly Hills, California. The cell phone number listed might be a place to start.

He pulled out his own cell phone and started to dial the number, then stopped, remembering why he'd come here in the first place. While looking for Iris's hotel room key, he'd come across the photo of her friend in the front pocket of her purse. He'd snapped a shot with his phone, figuring he could show it around, help her out.

Not as if he had much else to do these days.

He showed Claudell the image. "Ever seen this woman?"

Claudell peered at the photo. "Not me. Pretty, though. You meet you a girl, Mad Dog?"

Maddox ignored the bartender's salacious grin. "She's gone missing from the Hotel St. George."

"St. George?" Claudell's smile faded. "No good. I hear bad thing about St. George."

Maddox pocketed his phone. "What bad thing?"

"People gone." He snapped his fingers. "Like that."

"What do you mean?"

Claudell picked up another glass and started polishing. "A man go into the Tremaine yesterday. Say his friend missing from St. George. Gone, nobody know where."

Maddox hadn't heard about it. "Did he talk to the police?"

Claudell made a face. "They want it go away." He lowered his voice, as if imparting a deep, dark secret. "There more."

"More disappearances?"

Claudell nodded. "Bad thing happen at St. George. You smart, you stay away." The telephone sitting at the end of the bar began ringing. Claudell went to answer it.

Maddox looked down at Sandrine's image on his cell phone. *Where'd you go, darlin'?*

The bartender wasn't what he'd call a reliable source; his integrity was questionable, and he was a sucker for a spooky story. But if Iris's friend Sandrine wasn't the only person to go missing from St. George—

His cell phone vibrated against his palm. The display panel popped up, showing an unfamiliar number. Maddox slid off the bar stool and headed outside, pushing the connect button on the phone. "Yeah?"

"Is this Mr. Heller?"

Well, hell. "Who's askin'?"

"My name is Charles Kipler. My client Celia Shore wants to thank you for your aid to her this morning."

"I think you must have the wrong guy."

"You weren't the man who gave aid to an injured woman on the beach earlier this afternoon?"

He ought to deny it. Save himself the headache. But there were a lot of unanswered questions about the woman on the beach, or more specifically, Iris's connection with her, that piqued his curiosity. "That was me. How did you get my number?"

"I'll explain later. Ms. Shore wants to see you. She's at St. Ignacio Hospital. I'll meet you in the lobby and take you to her room. How soon can you get here?"

"You expect me to drop everything and come visit your client, and you won't even tell me how you got my number?"

"Yes."

Frowning, Maddox tightened his grip on the cell phone. "Isn't she a little busy undergoing treatment or something?"

"She's been released to a room to recover. She's doing as well as can be expected under the circumstances."

Maddox quelled the urge to ask just what those circumstances might be. This guy might be a jerk, but he'd known just what buttons to push to make Maddox too curious to resist the request. He could poke around for answers once he was face-to-face with this Celia Shore. "I need to change clothes. I can be there around two-thirty."

"I'll be in the lobby waiting."

"How will you know it's me?"

"I have a photo of you." The man hung up before Maddox could respond.

He snapped his phone closed and rubbed his forehead, where the day's tension was beginning to form a painful knot right between his eyes.

Where had the man found a photo of him? He didn't make a habit of posing for snapshots. Although it was possible, he supposed, that someone on the beach had used a photo phone just as he had in Iris's hotel room.

The more important question was, who was Celia Shore and why did she want to talk to him?

THE PHONE on the hotel bedside table rang while Iris was dressing after a long shower. She grabbed the receiver, hoping Sandrine would be on the other end of the line with a crazy explanation for where she'd been.

But it was the hotel front desk. "There's a letter at the front desk for Miss Beck," the concierge explained in his crisp British accent. "Shall I send a porter with it?"

"Please." Iris finished dressing in a hurry and dug in her handbag for money to tip the porter. He arrived within five minutes and traded a creamy linen envelope for the cash. Iris locked the door behind him and opened the envelope, hoping the contents would give her a clue to Sandrine's whereabouts.

A rectangular card with embossed edges lay inside the envelope. "You and a friend are invited to a cocktail party in the Paradise Room at Hotel St. George," she read. The date listed in shiny silver ink was today's date. Eight o'clock.

The invitation requested an RSVP and listed a cell phone number. Iris picked up the phone and dialed the number.

A woman with a Midwestern accent answered on the first ring. "Cassandra Society."

Iris paused. Cassandra Society? What was the Cassandra Society?

"Hello?" the voice repeated.

Iris cleared her throat. "Hi. I received this invitation to a cocktail party tonight in the Paradise Room."

"Will you be able to attend?"

"Do you mind telling me how many people you expect to attend?" Crowds in close quarters were a nightmare for her these days.

"Sixteen invitations went out. We've had twelve people confirm so far."

A maximum of thirty-two people. In a private hotel meeting room, a number that size should be bearable, she decided. "Yes. I'll be there."

"Your name?"

"I'm calling for my friend. Sandrine Beck."

There was a brief pause on the line, punctuated by the sound of papers rustling. "You must be Iris Browning."

Iris dropped onto the edge of the bed, surprised. How did this woman know her name? "Yes."

"Sandrine mentioned you'd be here today. I hope we'll see you at the seminar tomorrow, as well?"

Seminar? What in the world had Sandrine gotten her into? She licked her lips and took a plunge. "I'll be there."

Wherever *there* was.

She hung up the phone and stared at the balcony door across from the bed, her mind racing to catch up with the chaos of clues she'd just received about her friend's whereabouts.

Seminars meant a conference of some sort. That would be easy enough to establish. She picked up the phone and called the front desk. The concierge answered.

"This is room two-twelve. I believe the Cassandra Society is holding a conference of some sort in this hotel, correct?"

"That is correct. Is there a problem?"

"No. No problem. Can you tell me anything about the Cassandra Society? What's its focus?"

The concierge hesitated before answering. "I believe that information is covered in their conference brochure, madam. Shall I have someone bring you a copy?"

"Yes, thank you. That would be very helpful."

"You are most welcome. I'll send someone presently."

She thanked the concierge again and rang off. Within a couple of minutes, there was a knock on the door, and a bellman handed over a tri-fold brochure printed on dove-gray paper. The title was printed in clean black type: Expanding Horizons: The Third Annual Conference of the Cassandra Society.

Iris opened the brochure and scanned the contents. Most of the language was carefully chosen to portray the Cassandra Society conference as scientific inquiry, but the bottom line was, the conference catered to people interested in psychic phenomena. That made sense, given the organization's name. Cassandra obviously referred to the heroine of Greek mythology whose prophecies were fated never to be believed.

The conference was exactly the sort of thing that would interest Sandrine. She was a medium herself and liked to study paranormal phenomena. It also explained why she'd have signed Iris up without giving her any forewarning. Sandrine knew Iris's ambivalence about going public with her abilities. She'd probably guessed—correctly—that Iris would've refused to come had she known about the conference.

She read through the brochure, looking for more information about the organization, but most of the text inside outlined the conference schedule and speaker bios. There was almost nothing about the Cassandra Society itself.

She sat on the edge of the bed, wishing she'd brought her laptop computer from home. If there'd ever been a time for a Web search, it was now. There had to be more detailed information about the Cassandra Society on the Internet than she was finding in this oh-so-uninformative brochure.

She finger-combed her damp hair away from her face and crossed to the closet where she'd deposited her luggage without unpacking yesterday afternoon. The second luggage rack in the closet sat conspicuously empty, reminding her that wherever Sandrine had gone, she'd taken her bags with her.

Pushing away a wave of despair, Iris unzipped the garment bag that contained the two dressy outfits she'd brought with her. The cinnamon-red silk dress was a little longer than the natural linen sheath and would hide her skinned knees. She pulled it from the bag and smoothed the sleek skirt. It would work for the cocktail party.

Meanwhile, she had just a few hours to research the Cassandra Society before the party.

MADDOX STARTED undressing as soon as he stepped inside his squat little bungalow nestled at the outer edge of the rain forest north of Sebastian. The house wasn't much to look at, but the view from his back veranda was worth every penny he'd spent on the place. Mount Stanley, the dormant volcano that had formed the island of Mariposa centuries ago, had long since transformed to a lush, blue-green peak towering over the tiny Caribbean island. Its southwestern face filled his panoramic view of the rain forest that spread, thick and teeming with wildlife, as far as he could see.

He didn't let many people in town know about this place. It would raise too many questions about where he got the money to buy a decent-sized house with a spectacular view on an island where land and housing were at a premium. Even inland places such as his cost a small fortune, a fortune a jack-of-all-trades beach bum like Mad Dog Heller shouldn't have at his disposal.

He'd created his life from scratch on the island. Well, from scratch and occasional dips into a massive trust fund that had sat in a bank accruing interest from when his father had died and left him his fortune eight years ago.

The old man hadn't bothered to acknowledge him before that. Married, rich and successful, he probably would never have admitted paternity if he hadn't gotten sick of his legitimate kids and their profligate spending and left Maddox half his fortune to spite them.

The money was still there, for the most part. Maddox had spent some of it, early on, taking care of his mother. But she'd died two years after his father, and he'd left the money mostly untouched since then.

When he decided to make the move to Mariposa, he'd brought nothing but the clothes on his back and the ancient Steinway upright piano that had been his mother's.

He showered quickly, taking time to shave the shadowy thatch of beard darkening his jawline. Toweling dry his hair, he booted up his laptop computer and typed in a search for "Celia Shore."

Scores of hits came up immediately. The first link read Celia Shore—Official Web site. He clicked it and the Web site loaded a splash of vibrant pinks and teals. Across the top of the page was a photo of a beautiful blonde in her thirties. A radiant glow of pearl pink edged the image. To her right, her name was written in looping cursive, with a line of narrow, straight type below: Psychic Healer.

Well, hell.

Chapter Three

"Are you calling from Mariposa? Is something wrong?"

Tears stung Iris's eyes at the sound of her sister's concern. "Yeah, Lily, there is." She told her older sister, Lily McBride, what she knew about Sandrine's disappearance, including the Cassandra Society. "Ever heard of it?"

"No, I haven't."

"I need to find out more about who they are and if they're somehow connected to what's happened to Sandrine. You got a minute to do an Internet search for me?"

"Don't start playing Nancy Drew with this, Iris. Take the next flight home and let the police handle it."

"They're *not* handling it, and I don't think they will unless there's someone here to push them into it. I have to stay, at least a few more days. I'll be careful, I promise."

"No, you won't. You never are."

Iris couldn't blame Lily for thinking so; she'd always had an impetuous streak to go along with her insatiable curiosity. But the last couple of years had taken a toll on her impulsive tendencies. She couldn't afford to take too many chances; her body wouldn't hold up.

But Lily didn't know that. Iris hadn't told either of her sisters just how bad the pain had become. Her younger sister, Rose, was still a newlywed who deserved a little uninterrupted happiness, and Lily was eight and a half months pregnant with her first child and didn't need any added stress.

Iris couldn't burden either of them yet. Not until she figured out how to stop the pain from rendering her an invalid.

"Lily, please. I just need you to do a quick Web search."

Lily exhaled audibly. "Cassandra Society, you said?"

"Thanks. I'll call you back in ten minutes."

TEN MINUTES LATER, Lily told Iris all she'd found, which was next to nothing. "It's mentioned on a few paranormal Web sites, but none of them really say much about the society and what it's about. Do you want me to read what the pages say?"

"No, thanks," Iris said, hearing weariness in Lily's voice. "How's McBride Junior?" The baby Lily was carrying was a boy.

"Playing soccer with my bladder as we speak."

The joy in her sister's voice brought tears to Iris's eyes. She didn't begrudge Lily a minute's happiness—God knew, she'd earned it—but she couldn't help feeling sorry for herself at the same time. Her sisters had found something she'd begun to fear she could never have in her own life.

She cleared her throat. "Lily, I'd better go—"

"Please reconsider catching the next flight out of there."

"Just a few more days, Lil."

Lily sighed. "All right. I'll see if McBride has ever heard of the Cassandra Society. Okay?"

"Okay." Her brother-in-law was a policeman. If the Cassandra Society wasn't legit, he might know about it.

"Just stay safe, okay?" Lily said. "It's bad enough that Rose has gone all crime fighter on us—"

"Love you, Lily. Talk to you soon." Iris rang off, tucked her phone in her purse and slumped on her bed, glancing at her travel alarm clock. Almost two. Still plenty of daylight left if she felt like venturing out for another round of "Have you seen this woman?"

Or maybe she could start looking for an Internet café and look up more on the Cassandra Society herself.

MADDOX SLUMPED BACK against his desk chair, his eyes narrowing as he read through Celia Shore's bio and a rundown of her claim to psychic fame. She listed several mid-tier actors as satisfied clients, and her photo page included images from television and red carpet appearances.

What the hell did a woman like that want from him?

He glanced at the clock over the piano. Just after two. He'd been in Mariposa long enough to adjust to living on island time, but somehow, he didn't think the same could be said of Mr. Charles Kipler. If he wanted to reach the hospital by two-thirty, he had to get moving.

He was tempted to call back and blow it off. But he couldn't shake the feeling that meeting Celia Shore was important.

He'd learned long ago not to ignore his instincts.

IRIS NEVER IMAGINED she'd have reason to contact "Mad Dog" again. But her search for an Internet café with computer terminals for rent was proving fruitless. Half the people she asked gave her blank stares, and the others had no clue where she could find such a place.

At her next stop, a chocolate-skinned waitress with a Dutch accent couldn't help with her search for an Internet café, but her interest perked up at the mention of Maddox's name. "You want to find Mad Dog, go talk to that crazy Claudell at the Beachcomber. He knows everything. But don't fall for his lines. Mad Dog's, either." The waitress gave Iris directions to the bar.

Outside, the sun had dropped lower, shadows lengthening across the busy streets of Sebastian's commercial district. The day's heat was fading, cooled by the fragrant ocean breeze.

A sudden gnawing sensation fluttered through Iris's chest. Emptiness, as if someone had scooped out her insides and left her body hollow. She tried to sense what direction the feeling was coming from, but it was faint and fleeting.

She looked around her, keeping her movements slow and calm. There were pedestrians moving all around her, tourists and locals alike, alone or in pairs or groups. Black faces, brown faces, people with tropical tans, people with bright pink sunburns and people with milky-white skin dotted with freckles.

A tall redhead wearing a straw hat to hide her pale complexion approached, deep in conversation with a shorter woman with mousy brown hair tucked up under a baseball cap. They passed Iris, leaving a cloud of jasmine in their wake. A broad-shouldered man with sandy hair and a Vandyke goatee lounged against a building nearby, talking on a cell phone. The emptiness nibbling at her insides could be from any of them.

She ignored the sensation and headed for the Beach-comber, where the waitress said she could find Claudell.

By the time she reached the Beachcomber, her feet were beginning to hurt and the sunscreen she'd applied before leaving the hotel was nearly melted off by perspiration. Her head was pounding, her knees stinging beneath the Band-Aids, and the full spectrum of human misery surrounding her here in the throbbing heart of paradise had weighted down her aching shoulders with an invisible rucksack.

The bartender looked up when she entered the mostly empty bar. He started to look back down at the shot of whiskey he was pouring but did a comical double take at her approach.

Without looking, he slid the shot glass down the bar to a dreadlocked man sitting at the end and wiped his hands on his apron. "What can I get you?" he asked.

"A bottle of water and some information," she answered.

FOR HIS TRIP to the hospital, Maddox had donned a pair of khaki chinos and a navy golf shirt picked up on his last trip to Miami, his concession to civilization, and tied his shoulder-length mop of sandy hair into a ponytail at the base of his neck.

It had taken him five minutes to reach St. Ignacio Hospital and another five to find a parking space within sight of the tiny security kiosk. The Harley-Davidson Road King was his baby, and he didn't like leaving it out in a public parking lot where anyone could jack it. But a twenty passed to the guard in the kiosk would ensure the Harley would be sitting there waiting for him when he got back.

Money well spent.

A dark-haired man in an Italian silk suit far too heavy for the tropics stood in the hospital lobby when Maddox entered, his arm lifted in the act of checking his watch. Had to be Charles Kipler, Maddox thought. He had lackey written all over him.

He stepped forward as Maddox approached. "Maddox Heller?"

"Charles Kipler?" Maddox mimicked Kipler's imperious tone.

Kipler's lips flattened into a thin line. "Follow me."

"You might want to add a pretty please to that."

Kipler, who'd already moved toward the elevators, turned to look at Maddox. "Do you have an issue with me?"

An issue? Maddox stared at the man. Did people really talk like that? "I'm here for me. Not for you or for your psychic friend."

Kipler's expression shifted at his use of the word *psychic*. "I suppose this is your way of saying you want some sort of compensation."

Maddox bit back a laugh. "No. This is my way of saying I'd like to know what your client wants with me."

Kipler sighed. "I don't know. She asked me to track you down and bring you here, so that's what I'm doing."

"Don't worry, Chuck. I'm sure you'll get some sort of compensation." Maddox clapped the agent on his shoulder and crossed to the elevators.

Kipler joined him as he waited for the car to reach the

lobby. Maddox slanted a look toward the manager, whose face had reddened. Most of Maddox's irritation faded into pity for the man. It was hard, catering to the whims of someone who held your livelihood in her hands. He'd seen a lot of men and women play that role in his so-called father's life—including his mother. There were always people willing to linger around the perimeter, waiting for crumbs to drop.

But it wore on a fellow.

"How's she doing?" Maddox asked as they stepped into the elevator and began the ascent.

"Well enough. She has a concussion and some abrasions."

Maddox could tell by Kipler's tone that something else was wrong. "Did she tell you what happened to her?"

Kipler eyed him warily. "That's still being investigated."

The elevator stopped on the third floor. The door opened and Kipler stepped out, turning right.

Maddox caught up with him, falling into step. "What aren't you telling me, Chuck?"

"The name is Charles."

"What aren't you telling me, Charles?"

Kipler stopped in the middle of the corridor and turned to look at him. "She doesn't remember what happened. She doesn't even remember arriving here on Mariposa. Her last memory is of the airport in Miami."

"Because of the bump on her head?"

Kipler didn't answer right away, gazing down the hall. "The doctor doesn't think the injury should have been enough to cause amnesia," he finally admitted in a hushed voice.

"Which means what?"

Kipler's gaze swung around to clash with his. "Are you a reporter?"

Maddox frowned. "No."

"You certainly ask a lot of questions."

"I like to be prepared." Maddox lowered his voice as well. "I'm here out of the kindness of my heart, because your client wants to talk to me. And because right now, I don't have a good reason to say no. But it won't take much to change that."

Kipler glanced down the hall again. "Promise me you won't upset her."

"I don't plan to."

Kipler's mouth tightened again, but he didn't respond except to motion Maddox to follow him down the corridor. They stopped in front of a closed door with a brass plaque engraved with the number 312. "She said to send you in alone." Kipler looked queasy, obviously not happy about that directive.

Maddox entered the hospital room. It was a semiprivate room, all the hospital offered, but the bed nearest the door was empty. He crossed to the second bed, where Celia Shore lay propped on pillows, bandages wrapped around her head and wrists. The bed sheets hid her ankles but he guessed they were probably bandaged, as well. Her eyes were closed, her expression placid, but Maddox was pretty sure she wasn't asleep.

"Tryin' to read my mind?" he murmured.

Her eyes opened slowly. "Just resting."

And trying to present a pretty picture to the grubby islander, Maddox added silently. He hid his cynicism and pulled up the armchair stashed in the corner of the room. "Your cabana boy said you wanted to see me."

Her lips quirked. "I take it Charles didn't make a good impression?"

He ignored the question. "I hear you can't remember how you ended up on the beach."

"I remember nothing since transferring planes in Miami."

"Mr. Kipler traveled with you?" He tried not to imply anything with the question.

"We had business to discuss."

And a phone conference just wouldn't do, Maddox supposed, getting a little clearer picture of the kind of woman he was dealing with. "What would you have done if Chuck out there hadn't been able to make it?" Maddox asked.

"That wasn't a possibility."

Maddox felt sorry for Charles Kipler all over again.

"What I came here to do was business-related. I wanted Charles nearby if I needed him. That's what he's paid for." Celia gave him a pointed look. "You don't have to approve."

The woman might or might not be psychic, but she was perceptive. He'd been trying hard not to show his distaste for her attitude. "Fair enough. Unlike Chuck, I *don't* have to be here, though. So tell me what you wanted to tell me and we can be done."

"I saw you leaving with a woman this morning at the beach. I need to know how to contact her."

Maddox sat back in the chair, surprised. "Why?"

"I wanted to thank her for her aid this morning."

Maddox wasn't quite buying that excuse, but he played along. "I don't know her that well. She's a tourist."

"You normally put your arm around tourists you don't know well?" Celia arched a perfectly plucked eyebrow.

"The heat got to her. I helped her get somewhere cool."

"Aren't you the Good Samaritan?" The other well-shaped eyebrow rose to join the first. "Where'd you take her?"

"I'm not at liberty to supply you with that information."

"I can make it worth your while."

He chuckled. "Lady, I'm not for sale. Tell you what I'll do, though. I'll try to find her for you and tell her you want to see her. Then it'll be up to her. That work for you?"

He could tell she wasn't entirely pleased. Probably wasn't used to being at the mercy of other people's whims. But she finally nodded her assent. "I'll be released from the hospital tomorrow. If I don't hear from you or your tourist friend by then, I'll have Charles contact you with our location."

"So you're staying on the island?" he asked, surprised.

"Yes. I came here for business. I intend to keep to my schedule as much as possible."

Maddox stood. "Well, I really am glad you're feelin' better. I hope the police can find out what happened to you."

"Thank you. And despite what you seem to think, I am grateful for your help this morning." She turned her head toward the window and closed her eyes, ending the conversation. He took the hint and left the hospital room.

Outside, Charles Kipler was pacing in front of the door. "Everything okay?"

"Everything's spiffy, Chuck." Maddox gave a polite nod and headed for the elevators.

Out in the parking lot, the Harley was where he'd left it. The guard in the kiosk gave a wave, and Maddox waved back before straddling the bike and strapping on his helmet.

He headed south toward the St. George, trying to figure out how to approach Iris the Jet-lagged Tourist with Celia Shore's request. From what little he knew of Iris, she'd probably volunteer to camp out in the woman's room just in case she needed help. Fortunately, he could assure her that Celia had Chuck the Cabana Boy to fetch and carry.

Maybe he was wrong about Iris. Maybe her friend had finally turned up and Iris was out on the beach right this minute catching some sun. Maybe she wouldn't give a damn that Celia Shore wanted to talk to her.

But his gut told him he wasn't wrong. Iris had Goody Two-shoes written all over her.

As he slowed at a crosswalk on Seville Street near the club district, he heard someone call his name. He turned and saw Claudell standing in the doorway of the Beachcomber.

"Mad Dog!" Claudell flapped a bar towel at him to get his attention.

Maddox drew the Harley to the curb. "What now, Claudell?"

"Woman come lookin' for you. Name Iris."

Anticipation fluttered through Maddox's chest, catching him by surprise. Ignoring it, he pulled off his helmet. "You didn't take any of her money, did you?"

"No, sir. I figure you wanna see a pretty girl like that. I tell her you probably at the Tropico."

"Damn it, Claudell, you sent that girl to the Tropico?" Anxiety washed into Maddox's gut on a wave of acid.

"You know them guys not gonna give her no trouble. She safer down there than up at the Tremaine."

Claudell was wrong. Iris wasn't safe alone anywhere, not in her fragile condition. "If she gets hurt, I'm comin' after you, Claudell."

Stomach clenching, Maddox whipped back onto the street, weaving through the haphazard traffic congesting Seville. A couple of blocks down, he took a left, heading into a seedier part of the club district.

FROM THE OUTSIDE, the Tropico looked like a dive. Flaking paint on the clapboard facade suggested that at some point, the place had been painted a lively mango-yellow, but the color had long since faded under the tropical sun. A single wood door sagged off-kilter in the storefront, about as un-inviting an entryway as Iris had ever seen.

Figured a guy like Maddox would frequent a place like this.

The street was dark and growing darker, a dilapidated two-story building across the street casting shadows on the scene. A glance at her watch told her it was nearly four. She was running out of time before the cocktail party. Taking a deep breath, she opened the sagging door and stepped inside the bar.

The bar's interior looked as disreputable as the outside. A scuffed wooden bar took up the far end. Rickety shelves lining the walls behind the serving area were laden with dusty, half-full bottles that looked to be on the verge of tumbling off the shelves and shattering on the grungy concrete floor.

Several customers—all men—turned at the sound of

the door opening. Most of them wore jeans and faded T-shirts stretched over bulging muscles or bulging bellies. Tattoos darkened their arms and necks and even faces.

It was a biker bar, Iris realized with a combination of fascination and dismay. Who knew there were biker bars in the Caribbean?

A large black man with a snake tattoo coiled around his neck stepped away from the billiard table wedged into a cramped space on the left side of the bar. "You lost, missy?"

She debated asking for Maddox, but he clearly wasn't here, and she didn't need to be here, either. "Must have taken a wrong turn," she murmured and backed out of the bar.

The empty feeling that had begun to fade as she approached the Tropico slammed into her chest the moment she stepped into the street. Reeling from the sensation, she groped for the wall, the rough clapboard scraping her palms. She slumped against the bar front, trying to regain her equilibrium.

"Miss?" The raspy masculine voice was tinged with a foreign accent.

She jerked upright, opening her eyes.

A pair of hazel eyes stared back at her from a craggy face only inches away. It took a second to realize she'd seen the man before. He was the sandy-haired man with the Vandyke beard she'd seen earlier outside the café, talking on a cell phone.

"What do you want?" she asked, apprehension clenching her heart.

The man bent closer, his voice dropping to a whisper. "I may know something about your missing friend."

Iris stared at him, suspiciously. Had he been following her? "What are you talking about?" she asked, feigning ignorance.

"My friend Hana Kuipers was at the St. George for the conference, too," he said. "She disappeared yesterday, just like your friend Miss Beck."

Iris couldn't tamp down a flutter of hope. But before she could speak, the door of the Tropico opened, and an enormous Mariposan biker emerged, his gaze moving immediately to the bearded man.

"You botherin' the lady?" The biker towered over the man.

The bearded man shook his head. "I'm just talking to her."

The biker stepped forward menacingly. "Go back to fancy town, Dutchman."

Iris slumped against the wall of the bar, overcome by the fierce anger coming from the biker. The bearded man looked her way, his eyes darkening. For the first time, the sense of emptiness around the bearded man disappeared, filled in by a flutter of emotion she thought might be concern.

She looked up at him, releasing a small hiss of surprise.

The emotion cut off immediately, as if she'd suddenly run headfirst into a brick wall. The bearded man's gaze shifted.

The biker lunged suddenly, driving the bearded man against the front wall of the bar. The impact made the clapboard rattle. As the biker reared back to deliver a punch, the bearded man rolled to the side in one nimble movement. The biker's hand slammed into the clapboard, splintering the wood. He yelped in pain.

Iris gasped as shattering pain sped through her hand. She pressed her fist into her belly, trying not to cry out.

The bearded man delivered a pair of vicious jabs to the

biker's kidney, grunting with satisfaction at the man's howl of pain. The biker slid face-first down the wall, landing on his knees. Iris fell with him, her back aching in sympathy.

The bearded man knelt by Iris. She stared at him, realizing he was no ordinary tourist. "Who are you?"

He didn't answer. The door to the Tropico was opening, about to spill a dozen of the Creole biker's comrades to join the fray. Somewhere down the street, a feral growl of a motorcycle approached, getting louder.

The bearded man gave Iris one last look and took off running.

Chapter Four

Maddox wasn't sure what he'd find when he reached the Tropico. Iris playing Florence Nightingale certainly wasn't it.

Yet there she was, kneeling next to Jacob Massier's crumpled body on the street in front of the biker bar, her hands moving over the biker's back while a small crowd of bar regulars gathered in a restive semicircle behind her. She didn't look up as Maddox pulled the Harley to a stop nearby.

He took his helmet off and started to ask what the hell she thought she was doing when he realized he'd seen the glassy-eyed look on her face once before, on the beach when she'd held Celia Shore's hand while they waited for the EMTs to arrive.

Jacob Massier stirred suddenly, pushing up on one elbow. Iris dropped her hands away from his back and fell sideways, slumping against the front wall of the bar. A murmur of confusion broke out among the gathered bikers, as if they weren't sure if they should go to her aid or leave her alone to recover from whatever was ailing her.

Maddox pushed past them and crouched by Iris,

lifting her chin to check her eyes. They focused slowly on him, a soft breath escaping her lips. "I was looking for you," she said.

"So I hear," he responded, lifting his fingers to her throat to check her pulse. She flinched at his touch, as if it hurt her. He dropped his hand away, satisfied that her pulse was strong and steady, and rocked back on his heels. "I thought you were going to take a long nap and let yourself recover."

"I was feeling better," she answered.

"Obviously not better enough." He offered her his hand. She eyed it warily.

"I don't bite. Unless you want me to."

She rewarded the hoary joke with a lopsided grin that went a long way toward easing the knot that had settled in his belly seconds after Claudell had told him where she'd gone. She took his hand, trembling as he closed his fingers over hers.

"Is he okay?" Her gaze slid past him to settle on Jacob, who'd made it to a sitting position.

"You okay, Jake?" Maddox asked the biker.

"I'm good," he answered gruffly, his expression betraying a hint of embarrassment. "Lady got the mojo."

Considering the way his stomach was fluttering just from the feel of her soft hand in his, Maddox couldn't argue.

"ARE YOU SURE you shouldn't be back in bed, resting?" Maddox scooted his chair closer to Iris, the spicy smell of him mingling with the chicory aroma of the coffee at her elbow. As she'd figured, he'd known where to find the only place in Sebastian with Internet-wired computers for rent.

"I want to know more about this Cassandra Society." Iris

typed the name into the search engine, hoping she'd have better luck than Lily had.

"I want to know more about the guy with the beard," Maddox muttered. "Tell me what he looked like."

She looked away from the computer. "Sandy blond hair and hazel-green eyes. His beard was trimmed Vandyke style, and a little darker than his hair."

"How old?"

"Late thirties, maybe older."

The Internet café was nearly empty, though with the dinner hour approaching, a few more people were beginning to filter in. Iris was glad they were mostly alone. The relative isolation had helped her recover from her experience at the Tropico. Only a twinge remained in the general vicinity of her kidneys, and the stinging sensation in her right knuckles was nearly gone.

"You said he had an accent?"

"Yes. Dutch, maybe. Or German." She turned back to the computer, glancing over the listings. As Lily had indicated on the phone, the Cassandra Society didn't appear to have a Web site, but the search engine had come back with a few links. She tried the first one and found herself on a self-help page full of paranormal psychobabble.

Great.

"When I showed Claudell a photo of your friend—"

"Where'd you get a photo of Sandrine?" she interrupted, looking up at him.

He pulled a cell phone from his pants pocket, aimed and pushed the button. A bright flash made her blink. "I took a picture of her photo while you were unconscious."

He scooted closer, showing her the photo he'd just snapped of her.

She grimaced at the deer-in-the-headlights look on her face in the photo, not liking the idea of him going through her things while she was unconscious.

"The picture was sticking out of your purse. I just grabbed it, took a quick snap with the phone and put it back in your purse."

"Why?"

"I figured I could show it around, see if anyone had seen her."

"I just don't understand your interest."

His silence drew her gaze again. This time, he was looking at the computer screen.

"You didn't finish what you were saying," she murmured. "Did your friend recognize Sandrine?"

He looked up at her slowly, his eyes narrowing. "No. But he'd heard about people going missing from the St. George."

Dread curled inside her. With growing alarm, she realized that at least some of the cold, clammy sensation she was experiencing was coming from Maddox.

How bad did a situation need to be to scare a man called Mad Dog?

"How many people?" She tried to read his expression, see if she could discern any more of what he was feeling, but his expression was shuttered. And she wasn't a mind reader.

"Claudell said more than one. And the man who approached you at the Tropico mentioned a missing friend."

"If he was telling the truth." She couldn't shake the memory of the empty sensation emanating from the

bearded man. He'd given off nothing. No fear, no pain—
except for one brief moment when he'd looked at her with
a quiver of concern that had quickly fled.

"Why do you think he wasn't? Because he ran?"

She shook her head, unable to explain her instincts
without going into details about her gift. "I just got the
sense he was hiding something."

Another wave of darkness washed through her, as if her
words had opened a floodgate of anxiety inside him. She
forced herself not to move away, but she couldn't quite
bring herself to reach out to him, either.

She'd always felt it was her duty to relieve pain where
she could. Otherwise, what meaning was there in having
a gift that took such a toll on her body and her spirit?

All she had to do was take his hand and the darkness of
his fear would flow out of him and into her. But she
couldn't do it. She felt too fragile right now. All her energy
had to be focused on finding Sandrine.

"I'll see what I hear at the party tonight," she said. "Surely
if other people have missing friends, there'll be talk." She
looked back at the computer and tried another link.

"I'll come by tonight, hang out and talk to some of the
hotel staff, see if they have any stories to tell about the conference," Maddox suggested. "If you need me at the party,
I'll be around. Just holler."

To her surprise, the familiar cadence of his Georgia accent
seemed to have a soothing effect on her rattled nerves. For
the past twenty-four hours, she'd felt as if she were navigat-
ing an alien world. Hearing the inflections of home in
Maddox's slow drawl eased her growing sense of isolation.

But letting herself become too accustomed to having Maddox around was its own kind of folly, she knew.

She sneaked a quick glance at him. He'd cleaned up better than expected, she had to admit, the khaki slacks and crisp navy shirt a definite upgrade from the faded T-shirt and denim shorts he'd been wearing when she first met him at the café that morning. His overlong hair was pulled back neatly, revealing the full impact of his masculine features and the dimples that appeared whenever he smiled.

But she knew enough about bad boys to know that Maddox was a lousy bet. He might be a fun fling—she'd put money on it—but he'd end up breaking her heart.

She didn't have much heart left to spare these days.

"I almost forgot why I was lookin' for you in the first place," he murmured, leaning closer to her. His breath stirred the tendrils of hair at her temple. "I went to the hospital to check on that lady on the beach."

She gave a small start of surprise. She should have checked on the woman herself, she thought, dismayed that it hadn't even crossed her mind. "How is she?"

"Doing well. You called it—mild concussion."

"Did you talk to her? Did she know what happened to her?"

He shook his head. "She doesn't remember anything after gettin' on the plane in Miami."

Iris shuddered at the thought. How horrible, to wake up in such a state and remember nothing about how it happened. "What's her name?"

He pointed to the computer screen. There, on the list of hits from her computer search, was a link to the official Celia Shore Web site. "Celia Shore, psychic healer," he intoned, obviously not impressed. "She wants to see you."

Iris frowned. "Why?"

He shrugged. "To say thanks, I guess."

"I didn't do anything."

"She seems to think you did."

A phantom memory of the injured woman's pain buzzed through Iris's nerves. "How long will she be in the hospital?"

"They'll probably let her go tomorrow if there aren't any changes in her condition."

Then maybe I won't have to see her, she thought, and immediately felt guilty. No matter what else Celia Shore might be, she was a woman who'd been assaulted and left on the beach to die. She was in pain, both physical and emotional, and Iris didn't have the right to judge whether she was worthy of comfort and relief.

But she didn't for a moment think the woman was actually a psychic. Iris knew what a real psychic looked like, how she behaved and the toll her special gift took on her. She'd seen it in her sister Lily's retreat from the world and the migraines she'd endured just to fight the visions that tortured her. In Rose's despair when the death veils had foretold the death of a friend. In her own ever-worsening pain whenever she tried to use her empathic healing gift to ease the suffering of others.

Real psychics didn't go to Hollywood and make a fortune holding the hands of overpaid, emotionally immature celebrities.

She forced her attention back to the Web search,

clicking through several of the links. As Lily had mentioned, the references to the Cassandra Society were generally in passing, but clearly the Cassandra Society was an organization dedicated to paranormal research. Of the self-consciously serious type.

Lovely.

"Guess that's why Celia Shore was in town," Maddox murmured, reading over her shoulder.

"Must be."

"Your friend too, huh?" He sounded almost apologetic, as if he pitied her for finding out her friend was involved with "those" kind of people.

"Sandrine is interested in the paranormal," she said noncommittally.

"So." He looked at her, trapping his lower lip between his teeth for a brief moment. "You goin' to the seminars tomorrow?"

She should. She'd find out a lot more about Sandrine and the Cassandra Society that way. But right now, the thought of it was more than she could bear. "I don't know."

"I could take you to the hospital to see Celia before she's checked out of there tomorrow. If you want."

"Only if you have a second helmet." The ride from the Tropico to the Sand Dollar Café had been one of the scariest experiences of her life.

He tucked a lock of hair behind her ear. "I'll drive the Jeep."

Her cheek tingled where his fingers brushed her skin.

He dropped his hand and looked away, but not before she caught a hint of consternation on his face, as if he realized he'd overstepped some sort of line by touching her that way.

Good. That meant he knew there were lines in the first place. It made it easier to take him up on his offer of help.

She spent another fifteen minutes reading through the links without learning much more about the Cassandra Society. Sipping the last of her coffee, she turned to Maddox, who sat draped over the chair beside her, watching her with lazy blue eyes that made her breath catch.

She licked her lips. "Thanks for showing me this place. I should head back now. The party's in a couple of hours."

"Sure you don't want a ride?" His cheeks dimpled with a slow smile.

"The walk will be good for me."

"Okay." He stood when she did. "I'll walk you back."

"That's not necessary—"

"I'll walk you back," he repeated firmly. He put his hand between her shoulder blades, nodding toward the door. He stopped to say something to the guy at the cashier's stand, handed him some cash and then led her outside.

"What about the Harley?"

"I paid that guy an extra ten to make sure it's here when I get back. Let's go."

THE DAY WAS WANING, the sun already low on the western sky, gilding the Caribbean Sea as it stretched toward the horizon. The sun was warm on her cheeks, and the air was fragrant with the tang of the sea. For a moment, Iris could almost believe she was on a tropical vacation with nothing to worry about but where to go for dinner.

Almost.

"Hungry?" Maddox asked as they neared the main drag. "There's a fish-and-chips stand just over there."

She was hungry, she realized. She took him up on his offer, waiting while he dealt with the street vendor and returned with two cardboard boats full of fried fish and crispy French fries.

"Careful, it's hot." He handed her one of the boats.

She gingerly plucked off a piece of hot fish ad popped it in her mouth. The blend of spices on the breading and the delicate flavor of the fish made her hum with satisfaction.

"Good, huh?" He nudged her with his shoulder, motioning with a nod of his head for her to follow him. They set off down the main street toward the beach, mingling with the other tourists strolling the boulevard.

BY THE TIME THEY REACHED the beach road, Iris proclaimed herself stuffed and handed off the rest of her meal to Maddox. She'd eaten less than half, he noted with some consternation, but the meal and the exercise had seemed to do her some good. There was a little more color in her cheeks and she didn't seem as weak as she'd been when he'd found her outside the Tropico.

"You must love living here in Mariposa." Iris turned to look at him, her eyes alight. He felt a tug in the center of his chest, as if she'd pulled a string wrapped around his heart. "Do you ever get homesick?"

"I used to." He tossed the remains of their dinner in one of the public trash bins lining the walkway. "I got over it."

Iris laughed. Maddox found his gaze drawn by the

low, throaty sound. Her eyes sparkled, lighting up her whole face from the inside. He found it hard to take a deep breath.

Why had he insisted on walking her home? Or hell, if he really wanted to ask a tough question, why had he followed her out of the café that morning in the first place?

A combination of curiosity and boredom could explain some of his interest. But not all of it.

"How'd you end up in Mariposa, anyway?" she asked.

"Took a right turn at St. Croix."

"Seriously."

"Seriously. I was heading toward Trinidad for Carnival and took a detour on a whim. I liked it here and decided to stay."

"How long ago?"

"A little over two years."

She looked surprised. "I would have thought you'd been here longer. Everybody seems to know you, and you seem to know everything about this place."

"I'm very adaptable. Who knows, I may decide next week to head on down to Trinidad after all."

"A real rolling stone, huh?"

"Something like that."

"Never gathering any moss?"

"Nasty stuff, moss." The words came out as a warning. One he hoped she'd heed.

Silence fell between them, not an entirely comfortable one, as they moved ever closer to the St. George's pale pink facade.

He broke the silence. "What about you, sugar? What do you do up there in Alabama?"

"I own a plant nursery and I also do some botanical research on medicinal herbs."

"Botanical research," he echoed. Little Miss Jet-lagged Tourist had layers to her, didn't she?

"I have a master's degree in botany," she explained. "Maybe one day I'll finish my PhD. Too busy for it right now. What about you? What did you do before you took a right turn at St. Croix?"

"This and that. Nothing special."

"It must be nice living in paradise year-round."

"Mostly," he agreed. "The weather's great."

As they reached the entrance of the St. George, Iris turned and looked up at him.

"Why are you doing this?"

He didn't follow. "Doing what?"

"Helping me out." Her dark-eyed gaze grew wary. "Do you expect something from me in return?"

He didn't know whether to feel insulted or mortified. "I don't expect anything from you, sugar. I'm just helpin' out a tourist in need."

"You make a habit of that?"

"You caught me on a good week. I'm between jobs."

"Oh." She licked her lips. "I don't have a lot of money with me, but I can get some from my room—"

He grabbed her hand. She made a soft sound of surprise. "I don't need your money. What do you think I am?"

"I'm sorry. I didn't mean to insult you." Her brow furrowed. "I just thought—"

"I know what you thought." He released her hand, looking away from her.

"I really am sorry," she said again, catching his hand with hers. He tried not to look at her, but the feel of her fingers, soft on his skin, drew him in. Her gaze was full of remorse. "You've been good to me today. I don't know how to thank you."

"You just did. Don't worry about it." He withdrew his hand, wishing he were anywhere but here with this woman.

"I should attend the seminar tomorrow, shouldn't I?" Iris asked.

"Maybe you'll find your friend there."

"Maybe."

"But you don't really think so."

She released a shaky breath. "She would have left me a message if she knew she was going to be away overnight."

"Are you sure she didn't?" he asked, wanting to smooth the frown from her pretty forehead. "Maybe it got misplaced."

Her expression shifted. "Maybe they sent the note to the wrong room. Why didn't I think of that?"

Her sudden look of excitement made his stomach hurt. "Don't get your hopes up. It's just something to look into."

"Maybe you're right." She started up the steps to the hotel entrance. "Thanks again for everything!"

He tamped down the urge to follow her inside. His good deed for the day was done, and then some. He'd told her about Celia Shore. He'd helped her find a computer so she could look up the Cassandra Society. Hell, he'd even tucked her into bed when she'd fainted on him.

And besides, he'd see her tonight at the cocktail party.

BY 7 P.M., Maddox had taken his second shower of the day, dressed in a pair of black trousers and a white dress shirt, and headed back to the Hotel St. George to put his plan for the evening in motion. And a big part of the plan had just pulled into the St. George's employees' parking lot.

"Milo!" Maddox pushed away from the wall and walked toward the barrel-chested waiter parking his scooter a few slots down from Maddox's Harley.

Milo Maroulis looked up cautiously. "Mad Dog. What you up to?" He kept moving toward the kitchen entrance.

Blocking Milo's path, Maddox pulled a pair of twenty-dollar bills from his pocket. "I need you to call in sick. I need inside the cocktail party going on tonight."

"Why?" Milo asked, his voice wary.

Maddox flashed the waiter a sly grin. "Why do you think?"

Milo looked surprised. "You're not gonna hit on one of them crazy people, are you?"

Maddox stood in the doorway to keep Milo from going inside. "I'll make it sixty. You can use my cell phone to call in."

Milo pursed his lips. Maddox could tell he wouldn't put up a real fight; his eyes gleamed with unconcealed eagerness to take the money and run. Maddox added an extra twenty to the two bills in his hand and waved them in front of Milo.

Milo grabbed the bills from Maddox's hand and stuffed them in his pants pocket. "Go talk to Thomas. He knows you. Tell him I'm home with a sore throat and I asked you to take my place." Milo headed for the parking lot, a spring in his step.

Maddox entered through the kitchen, ignoring the

curious looks from the staff already assembling appetizers for the party. He snagged a spiced shrimp off one platter, flashing a smile at the pretty Creole sous chef, and went to look for the wait staff manager to talk his way into the cocktail party.

THERE HAD BEEN no note waiting for Iris in her box when she returned to the hotel that afternoon. She'd asked the desk clerk about the possibility of a mix-up, but the clerk had told her that nobody had mentioned getting the wrong note, so far.

She hoped the Cassandra Society cocktail party would offer more information about her friend's disappearance.

The Paradise Room didn't quite live up to its name. Though live potted palms dotted the room and the walls were painted in a gradation of red, coral and saffron in an attempt to capture the colors of an island sunset, the room was small and windowless, rendering the attempt at setting a mood kitschy.

The dozen or so people Iris found mingling in the Paradise Room didn't seem interested in the decor, however. They gathered in clusters of three or four, drinks in hand and deep in discussion.

She took a deep breath and entered the room. To her left, a long table lined the wall. A couple of women dressed in black business suits sat at the table. Half a dozen name tags lay in a neat row. The younger of the two women, a redhead with a round, girlish face, smiled at her. "Welcome, Iris."

Iris blinked at the woman's use of her name.

The redhead chuckled. "No, I'm not a clairvoyant. You're just the only person on the RSVP list I haven't met yet."

Iris recognized the woman's lilting Midwestern twang. She was the one who'd answered Iris's RSVP call.

Handing Iris her name badge, the girl added, "My name's Sharon Phelps. I'm with the Minnesota chapter. I'm a medium, I guess you'd call it. Dead people talk to me."

Iris tried not to gape. Though she'd lived her entire life knowing she had a special gift, she'd never spoken of it so openly and matter-of-factly with anyone outside her family. "Nice to meet you," she managed after a couple of seconds.

"What do you do?" Sharon asked as Iris pinned the badge to the front of her dress.

"I own a plant nursery," Iris answered automatically, then realized that wasn't what Sharon was asking. "And I, um…I guess I feel things."

"Like an empath?" Sharon asked brightly.

"Sort of," Iris conceded, the skin on the back of her neck burning. She had steeled herself all afternoon to handle the flood of human emotions that would surround her tonight, but she wasn't getting much from Sharon or the older woman at the table. It wasn't the same as the empty sensation she'd received from the bearded man outside the Tropico. It was just a sort of blandness, as if neither woman had a care in the world.

Must be nice.

"Well, I won't keep you. Go ahead and mingle. And try the stuffed shrimp—they're delicious." Sharon waggled her fingers in a goodbye wave, leaving Iris no choice but to turn and start working the crowd.

She spotted a woman sitting alone across the room. Safe enough choice, she thought. She took a deep breath and headed across the room, feeling exposed and vulnerable.

She wished Maddox were here, she realized with surprise. With Sandrine missing, he was the closest thing she had to a friend on the island.

If you need me at the party, I'll be around. Maddox's promise echoed in her head.

I need you, she thought. *Where are you?*

A sharp flood of dark emotion shot through her, trapping her breath in her lungs for a second. She faltered to a stop, gripping the back of a chair sitting next to an empty table. She pulled it out and sat, closing her eyes against the neon flash of emotion coloring her vision bright red.

Anger. Contempt. Rage.

As suddenly as she felt it, the emotion fled, leaving only a bitter residual sensation inside her.

She opened her eyes and found herself staring at the gold buttons of the waiter's jacket. "In the mood for a cheese cracker?"

Iris's head snapped up at the soft, familiar drawl.

The waiter was Maddox.

Chapter Five

Maddox grinned at Iris's look of surprise, pleased that he'd been able to pull off this investigative coup. It brought back a few of the better memories of his former life.

"How'd you manage this?" Iris selected one of the crackers and gazed up at him with an admiring gleam in her dark eyes.

"I know people," Maddox answered, deliberately cryptic. Desire fluttered in his gut, not unexpected but not particularly welcome. Iris Browning was a complication he couldn't afford. "Anything new on the Cassandra Society?"

"Not much more than we found online," Iris murmured, nibbling at the edge of the cracker.

"Same here. So, your friend Sandrine is the hoodoo sort?"

She frowned, apparently not happy with his characterization of her friend. "She considers herself a medium."

"Do you? Consider her a medium, that is?"

Iris looked down at the cracker. "She's very perceptive. More than the average person."

Lots of people are perceptive, he thought, *but they don't think they've got some special gift from the gods.*

"Reckon why she signed you up for this thing?" he asked.

Iris didn't answer. He started to repeat the question when he caught sight of a man gesturing at him from across the room. He sighed. "Duty calls. Go mingle."

He worked the room slowly, listening to snippets of conversation that gradually began to draw a clearer picture of what the Cassandra Society and the conference here at the Hotel St. George were about. As one plump, overearnest woman holding court in a group of five expounded, "It's about science, not magic, and it's time we prove it to the skeptics."

Good luck with that, Maddox thought, heading back to the kitchen for a new tray of appetizers.

In the kitchen, the pretty Creole sous chef, Darlene, flirted as he loaded the tray with coconut shrimp and stuffed mushrooms. "Anybody put the hex on you out there, Mad Dog?"

He flashed a smile. "Not yet, but the night is young."

"I hear they found that American psychic lady, Celia Shore, all beat up on the beach." Darlene leaned closer, lowering her voice to a half-whisper. "You'd think a psychic would've known the attack was comin'." She cackled at her own joke.

Maddox smiled, but his heart wasn't in it. He'd seen firsthand the kind of injuries Celia had sustained. She might be a big old faker, but she hadn't faked the scrapes and bruises on her wrists and ankles or the concussion she'd sustained.

Something bad was going on here at the Hotel St. George, something to do with the Cassandra Society.

And he intended to find out what.

IRIS'S FEET WERE ACHING, though the pumps she wore were low-heeled and ridiculously comfortable. She suspected most of the pain was a vicarious sensation from the short-skirted blonde standing next to her in a pair of spike-heeled strappy sandals. Iris was tempted to make an excuse to leave, but the blonde, a "sensitive" named Andrea Barksdale, seemed to know something about everyone in the room. So Iris ignored her aching feet, discreetly pumping Andrea for information.

"That's Trevor MacAllan." Andrea pointed to a tall, gaunt-looking man in an ancient tweed suit. "He has a show on British television where he goes to various haunted places and speaks to the dead. Really quite amazing the people he's spoken with. Ask him about his talk with William Shakespeare."

Why, Iris wondered, did celebrity mediums always have conversations with famous people? Never Joe Blow from Peoria who died of a heart attack while shoveling snow.

"Well, hello," Andrea said, her voice tinged with intrigue.

Iris followed her gaze. Near the entrance, a slender, well-built man in his thirties surveyed the room calmly. He was dark-skinned—Arabic, perhaps—with strong, even features. The stylish cut of his short black hair accented his striking bone structure. His dark eyes met hers, and he gave a polite nod.

"Who's that?" Iris asked Andrea when he looked away.

Andrea shook her head. "I don't know, but I'm damn well going to find out." She set her martini glass on a nearby table and crossed the room to greet the stranger.

For a moment, Iris watched Andrea pour on the charm,

feeling a little sorry for the newcomer. Turning her gaze back to the rest of the meeting room, she spotted Maddox a few yards away, gathering up empty glasses, his head cocked as he listened in on conversations. As if he felt her appraisal, he turned his head and shot her a conspiratorial look so intimate that it stole her breath for a moment.

We're in this together, that look seemed to say.

The sense of relief that flooded her in response caught her by surprise. She looked away quickly, annoyed at herself. *You're not in this together,* she scolded herself. *You're in this to find Sandrine, and if Maddox wants to help, you'll take it, but you're not a team.*

The pain in her feet, which had eased once Andrea headed across the room, was back. Iris turned her head to find the blond Canadian approaching, the swarthy stranger in tow.

"Iris Browning, this is Tahir Mahmoud. He's from Kazarastan."

"Kaziristan," Tahir corrected gently. He spoke perfect English, his accent British and formal. "Have you heard of it?"

"Of course. The embassy siege was only three years ago," she said softly. "I've kept up."

He laughed, reassuring her that she hadn't insulted him by bringing up his country's troubled past. "So you have. I assure you, the country has vastly improved in the interim. Miss Barksdale tells me that you're an American."

Iris took the hand he extended. The second his flesh touched hers, a sharp pain raced through the right side of her face, as if she'd just bitten the inside of her cheek. She couldn't suppress a wince, though she recovered quickly as the pain receded to a tingle. "Nice to meet you, Mr. Mahmoud."

Tahir released her hand. If he'd noticed her reaction, he didn't show it. "Please, call me Tahir. May I call you Iris? It's a lovely name."

"Of course. And thank you." Iris smiled politely.

"Tahir is an anthropologist," Andrea interjected, obviously not happy to be left out of the conversation.

"I am writing a book connecting the mystic traditions of my people with mystic traditions around the globe. When I heard of this conference, I knew I would have to attend."

"You consider this an exploration of mystic traditions?" Iris asked, both intrigued and skeptical.

"Traditions are continually recycled," Tahir answered. "One man's shaman is another man's medium?"

"Exactly." He motioned toward an empty table near the back of the room. "Shall we sit and discuss this further?"

Iris glanced at Andrea, whose sharp green eyes were focused on Tahir's face. *Safe enough to go with him,* she thought, *since we'll obviously have a chaperone.* "Certainly."

The three of them settled at the small, round table.

"Andrea tells me she is a sensitive," Tahir said. "Are you a sensitive as well?"

"I'm here in my friend Sandrine's place." Iris sidestepped the question. "Sandrine Beck. Do you know her?"

Tahir's brow accordioned with thought. "I am not familiar with the name, but there are so many people here."

"The name rings a bell with me," Andrea interjected. "What does she look like?"

Iris pulled Sandrine's photo from her clutch purse and

laid it on the table. Both Andrea and Tahir looked at it. Tahir shook his head, but Andrea nodded.

"I remember her. She was one of the focus groupers."

"Focus groupers?" Iris asked.

As Andrea opened her mouth to answer, a familiar drawl interrupted. "Canapés?"

Iris looked up at Maddox, who stood at her elbow with a tray of hors d'oeuvres. "No, thank you," she murmured, her voice tighter than she intended.

His eyebrow twitched upward as he offered the tray of appetizers to Andrea and Tahir. Tahir shook his head, but Andrea took a couple of stuffed mushrooms from the tray.

"Can I get you something to drink?" Maddox asked.

"I'm dying for another appletini," Andrea said. "Tahir?"

"Alcohol is forbidden by my religion," Tahir said, his tone gentle, as if to assure Andrea he was not offended.

"I can get you a Shirley Temple," Maddox drawled. "With a cute little cherry on top."

Tahir's gaze rose slowly to meet Maddox's. There was no humor in their ebony depths. "No, thank you."

"That'll be all, thanks." Iris glared at Maddox.

"Yes, ma'am," he murmured, moving on to the next table.

"Well, he was a bit fresh, wasn't he?" Andrea asked. "I suppose hotels can't always be picky about the help they hire."

Iris was surprised to find herself angered by Andrea's remark, given how annoyed at Maddox she'd been seconds before.

"He is not a native," Tahir murmured.

"He's been here awhile," Iris said without thinking.

When both Andrea and Tahir looked at her for further explanation, she realized she'd almost given away her prior connection to Maddox. "I noticed him talking with one of the other waiters earlier," she explained. "They spoke like old friends, so I assume he's been here awhile."

Her table companions seemed satisfied with her explanation, to her relief. She turned to Andrea. "You were saying something about a focus group before the waiter interrupted."

"Yes." Andrea nibbled around the edge of the stuffed mushroom. "Yesterday morning, after our first seminar session, Dr. Grinkov selected eight panelists and attendees to join him in an intensive focus group session."

"Are any of the focus group here tonight?" Iris asked.

Andrea looked around. "I don't think so. Your friend didn't tell you anything about the group?"

"I flew in yesterday afternoon. I haven't seen Sandrine at all. I'm beginning to worry about her," Iris confessed.

"Well, since I don't see any of the others, maybe they were moved to a different location for their part of the seminar."

Was the answer that simple? "Was Dr. Grinkov involved in any of today's seminars?" Iris asked.

"I didn't see him," Andrea said. "Tahir, did you?"

"I am sorry, I do not know him." Tahir touched Iris's hand, and a blast of darkness rocketed through her. She struggled to keep from jerking her hand away. Her whole body trembled with relief when he removed his hand.

She tried to read even a hint of the violent emotion she'd sensed in that brief contact, but his expression was placid. Had she mistaken someone else's feelings for Tahir's?

Maddox approached with an appletini. He set it in front

of Andrea. His gaze met Iris's, concern in his blue-gray eyes. "Can I get anything for you, ma'am?"

"I'd like a glass of water," she answered, surprised to hear her voice shake.

His brow furrowed, but he headed toward the kitchen.

Tahir leaned toward her, but thankfully he didn't touch her again. "Are you unwell?"

"You do look a bit pale," Andrea agreed, her tone a little too eager. Obviously, she wouldn't mind if Iris left her alone with Tahir Mahmoud.

At this point, Iris wouldn't mind it, either. What she'd just learned from Andrea could explain Sandrine's disappearance. She needed to find someone who could confirm the theory for her.

She glanced across the room, where pretty, red-haired Sharon Phelps from Minnesota sat at the reception table, talking to the older lady who'd been her companion all night. Maybe Sharon knew something about the special focus group.

"I think I'll make this an early night," Iris said, rising from the table. "Please give the waiter my apologies."

Tahir rose with her, bowing. "Delightful meeting you, Miss Browning. I hope to see you at the conference tomorrow."

She smiled but didn't make any promises. If Andrea was right, then all her worries about Sandrine might be unfounded, and she could relax and enjoy her island vacation.

She stopped at the reception table on her way out. Sharon smiled as she approached. "You're not leaving so soon, are you?" she asked brightly.

"I've been fighting off a headache all day," Iris fibbed. "I have a quick question before I go. What do you know about a focus group formed during yesterday's session? I believe a Dr. Grinko may have selected the participants."

"Dr. Grinkov," Sharon corrected with a smile. "Boris Grinkov. Brilliant man. He did a lot of early pioneering in parapsychology in Russia before the end of the Cold War. He's a bit of a psychic himself."

"Dr. Grinkov," Iris corrected herself. "Do you know anything about that group?"

"Dr. Grinkov sometimes takes special interest in certain people and their abilities. He has some theories about synchronized paranormality that are totally fascinating." Sharon's face glowed as she spoke of Dr. Grinkov, reminding Iris of a teenager waxing rhapsodic about a hot new boy band.

"So he might have selected some members of the seminar for a special experiment?" Iris didn't know whether to be relieved or alarmed by the idea.

"I'll be happy to ask the organizers for you. Let me see what I can find out tonight and get back to you tomorrow at the conference. If I forget, look for me, yeah? I'll be around."

"Thank you." Sharon's exuberant friendliness was beginning to wear Iris out, so she took her leave and headed for the exit.

"Your water." Maddox's voice stopped her midstep.

She turned to find him holding a bottle of water. "Thanks." She lowered her voice. "I have some information."

"Me, too. I'll tell you about it later." He handed her a bottle of cold water. "Who's the sheikh?"

There was an odd tone to Maddox's voice, a guardedness that she hadn't heard from him before. She glanced back at the table, where Tahir Mahmoud was taking his leave from Andrea Barksdale. "His name is Tahir Mahmoud. He's from Kaziristan."

A sudden jolt of darkness roiled through her, making her legs grow wobbly. She reached for Maddox's arm to steady herself, but touching him only intensified the feeling. She pulled back, gripping the nearby door frame.

"Are you okay?" Maddox started toward her.

She put up her hand to stop him. "Just lost my balance on these darned shoes."

His gaze dropped to her low-heeled pumps. He looked back up at her, his expression guarded. "Go rest. I'll check on you when the party's over."

She should tell him not to bother. She was tired. She had a killer headache starting to form at the base of her skull. Her feet still ached from feeling the pinch of Andrea Barksdale's spike heels, and the double shot of black emotion from both Tahir and Maddox lingered like nausea.

But when she spoke, she said, "Thanks. I'll wait up."

And kicked herself for it all the way back to her room.

MADDOX HANDED the last empty tray to Darlene in the kitchen. "The last folks are leaving. Need help cleaning up?"

She waved him away. "You know they'll kill me dead if I put a waiter on the cleanup. They don't wanna pay you the extra, Mad Dog."

"I'll do it under the table," he said, his sly grin rendering the offer risqué.

She grinned saucily. "Go on with your naughty self. I know better than to do the cha-cha with a fella like you."

He changed back into his street clothes in the employee bathroom and headed out the back to check on his Harley. It was still sitting, intact, in the parking lot. But knowing he was living on borrowed time, he flagged down the night shift security guard passing by on his rounds and slipped him a twenty to watch over the bike for the next few hours.

He rounded the side of the hotel, heading for the front, but stopped when he heard a familiar voice around the corner.

"It is not a good idea." Tahir Mahmoud's soft, clipped accent carried through the clear night air.

"I have no plausible reason to remain silent." The second speaker was also male, his voice pitched a few tones higher than Mahmoud's. He had a strong Russian accent. "What shall I say?"

"Nothing. I will take care of it." Tahir's voice grew softer, as if he was moving away.

Maddox turned the corner and spotted the Kaziristani and his Russian-accented companion, an older, rail-thin man in his fifties, walking up the steps to the hotel entrance. Maddox stayed in the shadows, watching them disappear inside.

He released a slow, unsteady breath.

A Kaziristani. Here. What were the odds?

He made himself keep moving, slowed his racing heartbeat to match the steady cadence of his footfalls on the granite steps of the hotel entrance. Inside, a blast of cool air dried the pearls of perspiration dotting his forehead.

Several guests milled about the lobby, some checking in, others taking advantage of the hotel lounge. Tahir Mahmoud and the Russian man were nowhere to be seen.

Maddox's heartbeat slowed further. The blackness filling his chest and gut began to recede.

Three years ago, he reminded himself. A lifetime.

It felt more like three minutes.

IRIS LAID the pencil on the desk and flexed her hands and wrists, gazing at the sketch of the bearded man with a critical eye. It was a good likeness, she decided, though it lacked something—the essence of who he was inside, perhaps, since she'd read almost nothing from him but emptiness during their brief encounter.

Still, anyone who had seen him would recognize him from the sketch. She'd show it around at the seminar in the morning, see if anyone knew who he was.

A sudden chill washed over her, sending goose bumps along her arms and legs. The cold slowly faded, replaced by a strange, jittery sensation that fluttered like a frantic moth.

A knock on her door made her jump.

She padded to the door and peered through the security lens. It was Maddox.

She unlatched the security chain and opened the door. Maddox stood with one hand on the door frame, his eyes hooded by his furrowed brow. "I'm not sure I should be here."

The raw honesty in his voice was a surprise. She was used to his glib, sexy-devil side. "Are you all right?"

He straightened slowly. Within the span of a second, the Southern bad boy was back. "Just a bad mood, sugar. I get that way when a bunch of suits order me around all night. Why don't I catch you in the morning?"

She touched his arm, steeling herself against the darkness she knew lurked inside him. "Why don't you come in for a minute and let me tell you what I learned?"

She didn't let go of his arm as she led him to the chair across from her bed. The nausea in the pit of her belly roiled, but she ground her teeth and held herself together, drawing the blackness out of him and into herself.

He looked up at her, confusion in his expression. The sensation pouring into her changed suddenly, the dark emotions eclipsed by a flood of relief.

She released his arm.

His gaze dropped. When he spoke, his voice sounded strange. Shaky. "What did you find out on your little reconnaissance mission, sugar?"

"There's a scientist who's the head of the Cassandra Society. Dr. Grinkov. He apparently pulled aside some of the conference attendees for a special focus group."

Maddox's head jerked up. "Dr. Grinkov?"

"Boris Grinkov. He's a former Soviet scientist whose field of expertise is parapsychology." She cocked her head. "Ever heard of him?"

Maddox's expression darkened. "I think I saw him."

"Dr. Grinkov?" she asked, surprised. "When? Where?"

"Just a minute ago, outside the hotel." A grim smile spread over his face. His eyes met hers, as dark as a stormy sky. "Talkin' to your buddy, Tahir Mahmoud."

Chapter Six

Iris frowned. "Are you sure?"

"Well, it was some older guy with a Russian accent. How many of those can there be around here?"

"Strange. Tahir said he didn't know Dr. Grinkov."

"People lie," Maddox countered. "Just because he bows and talks pretty doesn't mean a fellow's on the up-and-up."

She bristled. "I know that."

He dimpled, but the smile escaped his eyes. "I'm beginning to wonder if you do. I mean, here you are, all alone in your hotel room with a fellow you didn't even know before this morning. They could make you the poster child for what not to do when you're on vacation in a foreign country."

The danger she felt from Maddox had nothing to do with physical safety. "Should I call the police on you?"

His eyes darkened. "Probably."

The air around them sparked with tension. She forced her gaze away before she did something she couldn't take back. "Do you know Tahir Mahmoud?"

His long pause made her look up at him again. "No." He cleared his throat. "You said something about a focus group?"

Iris nodded. "Dr. Grinkov pulled several people into a special session yesterday. Nobody seems to know what the focus group was about, but Sandrine seems to have been one of them."

"Well, that's good news, isn't it?"

Iris bit her lip. "I want to think so. But why wouldn't she have left word for me if she was going to be out of pocket?"

"I don't know," he admitted. "But if all the others did that, too, I guess it explains all the talk about missing people huh?"

"What about you?" she asked Maddox, changing the subject. "Did you find out anything while you were playing waiter?"

"I confirmed that Celia Shore was part of this hoodoo shindig," he answered. "I think you ought to check in on her tomorrow after all. Maybe she knows something."

"I thought you said she had amnesia."

"She remembers everything before the flight here, so surely she knows why she was coming here in the first place."

"Okay."

He fell silent a moment, his gaze warm on her cheeks. She didn't look at him, afraid of what she was beginning to feel.

"What's wrong with you?"

Her head snapped up. "Excuse me?"

His voice was disarmingly gentle. "You're obviously in pain, but you said it's not gonna kill you. What is it, then?"

She closed her eyes. "It's just…pain. Sometimes bad, most of the time bearable. It's worse when I'm under stress." Nothing of what she'd just told him was a lie, exactly. She didn't think he was quite ready to hear that most of the pain she felt belonged to the people around her instead of herself. "I'm actually feeling better at the moment."

It was true. That unexpected flood of relief she'd felt during the last seconds of her connection with Maddox had eased the twinges and sensations left over from the party.

"I'm glad." He put his hand on her bare knee, his fingers warm and slightly callused. Instead of a repeat of the dark emotional pain she usually felt from him, raw, unfettered desire rocketed right to her core, stealing her breath.

It wasn't coming from him, she realized.

It was coming from her.

His emotions were calm by comparison. Gentleness. Concern. She felt a buzz of something else, a low-level tension that might be a faint echo of her own suddenly rampaging hormones, but his focus seemed to be more noble than carnal.

She rose to get away from him, needing the distance to calm her rattled nerves. She searched for a safe subject to get her mind off the fire licking at her belly. "I was hoping I'd see the man I ran into at the Tropico tonight at the cocktail party. He said his friend disappeared from the conference, too."

"Maybe she was part of that focus group, as well."

She supposed it could be true. His spoken concern for his friend had sounded real. But that emptiness—she couldn't shake the memory of that sensation. It was as if he had built a wall around his emotions, hid them so that she couldn't sense anything from him that he didn't want her to feel.

Could he know who she was, what she could do? But how?

"Are you sure he didn't tell you his name?" Maddox asked.

"Positive. But he mentioned his friend's name." She searched her memory, trying to recall the woman's name he'd mentioned. "Hana something—"

"There probably couldn't be that many people named Hana registered for the conference," Maddox noted, pushing to his feet. "I could check into that part of his story, at least."

"I'm not sure if they'll just give you information about hotel guests if you ask." Iris stood to walk him to the door.

"Well, I know ways of—" His words cut off mid-sentence as his gaze fell to the sketchpad on the table by the window. He picked up the pad, his brow furrowed. "Is this him?"

"Yes. I tried to sketch what I remembered about him."

"It's a good sketch." He sounded suddenly distant. "Can I borrow this?"

"Sure." She followed him as he strode quickly to the door. "Do you recognize him?"

He turned at the door to look at her. "He looks familiar. I'm going to show it around, see if anyone knows him."

"What about asking about this Hana?"

"I'll do that later." He was already halfway out the door.

"Maddox?"

He turned, his expression impatient.

"Be careful."

His dimples made a brief appearance. "Always am."

Then he was gone, jogging down the corridor and turning the corner out of sight.

WHEN AN AMERICAN CITIZEN needed help in a foreign country, he usually went to the U.S. embassy or consulate.

Most of the time, a diplomat worked out whatever problem a tourist might encounter, but for Maddox's purposes, a diplomat was useless.

He needed a security guy.

In Mariposa, the Regional Security Officer at the U.S. consulate was an agent in his midthirties named Nicholas Darcy. The son of a former U.S. diplomat to the United Kingdom, he'd spent the first twenty-two years of his life in London, attending Cambridge University and acquiring a British accent that subsequent years in the United States, training and working as a Diplomatic Security Service agent, had failed to eradicate.

Darcy had been a ladder climber at the DSS from the get-go, annoying his fellow agents in the worst way possible—by being better at his job than anyone else. Still, everyone, including Maddox, had to concede Darcy was damn good at what he did.

Unfortunately, that posed a problem for Maddox. What he needed was a guy who could be enticed to spill his guts for the right amount of money. Nick Darcy didn't fit the bill.

But he *was* the guy who could tell Maddox what he needed to know about the bearded man in Iris Browning's sketch.

Part of Darcy's job as RSO entailed the care and feeding of local law enforcement, who provided the RSO and his security staff with the necessary auxiliary support to keep the embassy or consulate safe from outside dangers. Maddox was hoping he'd find the RSO doing a little early-morning public relations work in one of the coffee shops frequented by Mariposa's finest.

Maddox was in luck. At the third diner he tried, he

found the tall, dark-haired RSO drinking coffee and sharing a plate of beignets with a couple of Sebastian cops.

Darcy looked up as Maddox approached, his expression shifting from watchfulness to surprise. "Heller."

Maddox smiled at the agent's look of barely veiled dismay. "Long time, no see, Darcy. Got a minute?"

Darcy's mouth pressed to a thin line of annoyance. In the native island patois, he asked the two local cops to excuse him and motioned for Maddox to join him at the cashier's kiosk. Darcy paid for his breakfast, as well as those of the Sebastian police officers, and led Maddox out into the warm morning air.

"What do you want?" Darcy asked as they walked toward the embassy complex a couple of blocks down the road.

"Information."

Darcy slanted a hard look at him. "I'm not in the information business."

"Of course you are." Maddox reached into his pocket and pulled out the folded sketch Iris had made the evening before. "I need you to answer something, for old times' sake."

Darcy stiffened. "We weren't mates, Maddox. I don't owe you anything for old times' sake."

Maddox tamped down the blackness coiling like a snake in his chest, gritting his teeth until the urge to lash out at Darcy passed. "Then how about for the sake of an American citizen in need? Or did you forget about your loyalty to your country and your fellow citizens while you were snarfing down the kidney pie in old Blighty all those years?"

Darcy stopped midstep and wheeled to face Maddox.

"You certainly know how to relate to people in positions of influence, Heller. I really have no idea why the Marine Corps thought you might be a liability."

Ignoring the taunt, Maddox thrust the sketch at Darcy. "This man accosted an American citizen yesterday. He spoke with a German or Dutch accent and told her that he could help her find her missing friend. Recognize him yet?"

Darcy looked at the sketch, a muscle in his jaw twitching. He looked up at Maddox. "What do you want?"

Maddox lowered his voice to a lethal half whisper.

"What I want to know, American citizen to American citizen, is what the hell the CIA wants with Iris Browning."

IRIS TOOK a deep breath and dialed the number to St. Ignacio Hospital. If she wanted to find out where Sandrine was, she couldn't afford to ignore any possible leads.

And Celia Shore could be a very important one.

The hospital receptionist patched her through to Celia Shore's room number. A male voice answered. "Yes?"

Iris cleared her throat. "I'd like to speak to Celia Shore. My name is Iris Browning. She asked to speak to me."

The pause on the other end of the line was so long that Iris thought she'd been disconnected. As she was about to hang up and redial, the man cleared his throat. "Who told you Miss Shore wants to speak to you?"

"His name is Maddox. I don't know his last name."

"It's Heller," the man said. "Maddox Heller."

Iris could tell the man didn't think much of Maddox. She stifled a smile. "Does Miss Shore want to talk to me?"

"I think she wanted to see you in person."

"I have a seminar this morning," Iris said, more quickly than she'd intended.

"You're attending the Cassandra Society conference?"

"Yes," she replied. "I understand Miss Shore was registered with the conference, as well."

"You should know that. She spoke the first afternoon." The man's voice deepened with suspicion.

"I didn't arrive until late the day before yesterday." Good grief, Iris thought, Celia Shore was just a celebrity psychic, not the president. The man's defensiveness seemed a little overdone. Then again, the woman had nearly been killed yesterday. A little wariness was understandable.

"Miss Shore will be released from the hospital today. She plans to rest today and then attend the rest of the conference beginning tomorrow. Are you staying at the St. George?"

"Yes."

"Miss Shore will be in touch." A soft click ended the conversation.

Iris hung up the phone with a sigh.

MADDOX HAD TO hand it to Nicholas Darcy. The RSO had a world-class poker face. "I have no knowledge of anyone from the CIA working here in Mariposa. Even if I did, I couldn't discuss it with a civilian." Darcy hit the final word a little hard; it was the only part of his pat answer that didn't sound as if it came straight from the diplomat's handbook.

"I don't exactly qualify as a civilian."

"Yes, you do." Darcy turned dismissively and started walking toward the consulate complex two blocks up the street.

Maddox caught up. "At least tell me if you've had any complaints about the Hotel St. George or an organization called the Cassandra Society."

Darcy turned his head at that, a frown creasing his brow. He started to speak but the trill of a cell phone interrupted. Darcy pulled out his phone. "Darcy." He listened for a moment. "Okay, I'll be there in five." He hung up. "I have to go."

"We're not finished here."

Darcy's cool gaze leveled with Maddox's. "Yes, we are."

Grimacing with frustration, Maddox folded the sketch Iris had made and stuck it in the pocket of his trousers. He pulled out his cell phone and tried Iris's room. No answer.

He hung up and straddled the Harley, taking a quick look at his watch. Almost nine.

Maybe she'd decided to go to the conference after all.

THE OPENING SESSION for the third day of the conference started at 9 a.m. Iris was waiting when the doors opened. She took a deep breath and entered the room.

Sharon Phelps and an associate sat at a small reception table at the front of the meeting hall. Sharon greeted her with a smile and handed her a name tag. "Hi again, Iris! I'm so glad you decided to join us for the sessions!"

"Thanks. Listen—did you get a chance to ask anyone about the focus group my friend is part of?"

"I'm pretty sure she and the others are probably at the Telaraña facility. It's Dr. Grinkov's research laboratory here on Mariposa. I've never been there, but I think it's somewhere on the eastern side of the island." Sharon lowered her voice. "I came across a list of the people who were invited to join the focus group." She pulled a sheet of paper from the notebook in front of her. "Don't tell anyone where you got this, okay?"

"I won't. Thanks." Taking the sheet of paper, Iris left the registration table. She glanced quickly at the list. There were eight names on the sheet. Sandrine's was there. So was Celia Shore's. But there was no one on the list named Hana.

She folded the paper quickly, tucked it into her purse and looked for a seat.

The conference room was set up with several tables lined up in rows. The handful of conference-goers who'd arrived early had scattered about the room in groups of two and three. Iris pinned on her name tag and took a seat by herself near the back. She opened the notebook she'd bought the night before in the hotel gift shop.

The few Internet references she'd found about the Cassandra Society had raised a lot more questions than they'd answered. She got that it was a group devoted to paranormal research, with a focus on science. But what were the seminars all about? Was it all lecture-oriented, or were the attendees supposed to interact or participate in experiments?

"Excuse me, is this seat taken?"

Iris looked up at the sound of a man's voice and found herself looking into the dark, mysterious eyes of Tahir Mahmoud.

"No, it's not taken," she said.

He sat beside her. "Iris, isn't it?"

She managed a smile. "Nice to see you again, Tahir."

A sudden wave of hostility filled her chest, as heavy as

dread. The soft scrape of chair legs on the floor drew her attention to her right, where Maddox Heller settled into the chair next to her. He gave her a polite smile, a warning in his eyes. She looked back to the front, trying not to show her surprise.

"Did you find your friend?" Tahir asked. "The one who was missing?"

She glanced at him. If Tahir was aware of the tension that Maddox's arrival had created in her, he didn't give any indication. "Not yet."

Tahir started rolling up the sleeves of his dress shirt. "I asked about the focus group Ms. Barksdale mentioned last night. Apparently Dr. Grinkov invited a small number of the conference attendees to form a special focus group off campus." He shrugged. "Perhaps your friend is there."

A sudden flood of blackness swamped her, so intense that she almost fell out of her seat. She clutched for Maddox's leg, digging her fingers in. Dark emotion coursed through her.

It was coming from Maddox.

She let go of his leg, turning her head slowly to look at him. He was staring at Tahir Mahmoud.

She followed his gaze and saw a burn scar on the inside of Tahir's left wrist. She looked back at Maddox, but he was staring forward, his jaw set.

The bitter taste of fear lingered on her tongue, but the darkness inside her eased, as if gathered up and buried away. She noticed a table along the side of the room where there were bottles of water lined up in a row.

She touched Tahir's arm. "I'm suddenly feeling a little

faint. I got too much sun yesterday. I think I'm still feeling the effects. Could I bother you to get me a bottle of water?"

"No bother at all," he assured her as he rose. He headed across the room to the refreshment table.

Iris turned to Maddox. "What are you doing here?"

"Crashed the party."

"Yes, I see that. What if you get caught?"

"I know the bouncer." He nodded toward the entrance, where a burly man with dreadlocks manned the door in a black suit. "Reginald Samuels, head of hotel security. Hell of a shindig to warrant guard duty by the head honcho."

"You know everybody." She glanced toward the refreshment table, where Tahir was selecting a couple of water bottles. "Why don't you tell me what you know about Tahir Mahmoud?"

"I told you, I don't know anything about him." Maddox's tone was casual, but some of the anger she'd felt from him earlier seeped into his soul from wherever he'd hidden it.

"No, you know him," she said softly, watching as Tahir turned from the table and headed back toward her.

"Shh. Can't talk now, sugar. Just pretend I'm not here."

Impossible, she thought, even if she weren't feeling every black thought he was thinking about Tahir Mahmoud. Maddox knew Tahir, all right. Hostility oozed from his pores.

Who was he? Why was Maddox denying knowledge of him?

Tahir reached her side and handed her a bottle of water. "Are you unwell? I could try to find a doctor—"

"No, I'm fine. Just thirsty, thank you."

Tahir sat beside her, his expression full of concern. But she didn't *feel* concern from him.

He wasn't a blank to her, exactly. She felt *something* coming from inside him. But it was sly and elusive. Impossible to pin down.

The seminar began a moment later, with a frizzy-haired woman dressed in a flowing black dress introducing her topic, the juxtaposition of science and historical myths such as vampirism, lycanthropy and angelic visitations.

Iris might have found the lecture mildly interesting, especially the section on herbology and its place in both science and myth, but she found herself too distracted by the tangle of sensations coming from Maddox to pay full attention.

She stole a glance at him and found him still staring at the scar on Tahir's wrist, his brow creased and his body tense.

What did the scar mean to him? It enraged him on some level—that much was clear—but it scared him, too.

To her relief, the lecture ended within an hour and the conference director gave them a thirty-minute break before the next session.

Tahir turned to her. "It has been a pleasure seeing you again, Iris. I hope we will see each other later." He gave a slight, formal bow and headed toward the exit.

As Iris started in the same direction, Maddox caught her by the wrist. "You're not following him."

She looked up at him. "What?"

"Tahir Mahmoud," Maddox said. "You're going to stay the hell away from him."

Chapter Seven

Iris pulled her arm away from Maddox's grasp. "I wasn't following him. But if I wanted to, I wouldn't let you stop me." She started walking toward the restrooms again.

Maddox caught up with her. "I don't trust him."

"Yeah, I get that," she said, not slowing down. "But I don't usually let other people tell me who I can be around."

He closed his hand around the back of her neck, pulling her to face him. "I know you don't really know me. I know I don't look like someone you'd want advice from. But I know trouble, and that dude's trouble. Stay the hell away from him."

"Funny. Someone told me the same thing about you."

She felt an old, dark pain pouring into her. Maddox dropped his hand from her neck, and the pain began to fade.

His eyes narrowed slightly. "Also good advice." He abruptly started toward the exit.

She let him go, despite a strange, pulling sensation in the center of her heart telling her to go after him and apologize. She'd hurt him with her careless words, hurt him in a way she hadn't been aware was possible.

Still, she shouldn't leave the seminar, should she? She had too many questions about Sandrine's disappearance, and the people in this room might be able to answer them.

She stared at Maddox's retreating back, unsure what to do.

So much for playing knight in shining armor, Maddox thought blackly, striding through the hotel lobby toward the exit. He'd gone above and beyond for Iris Browning.

Fat lot of good it had done him.

And now, thanks to the scar on Tahir Mahmoud's wrist, he couldn't walk away from Iris Browning, no matter how much she might want him to.

Three years and a whole lot of nasty water under a rickety bridge had passed since that August day when Kaziristani rebels with a group called al-Adar had laid siege to the American embassy in Tablis. Maddox had been off duty at the time, sleeping off a night shift guarding the embassy gate. It had gone down so fast, nobody had been prepared.

The aftermath had changed his life forever.

A lot of his memories of the day were painted in watercolor hues, blurred by time and adrenaline and fear. But the one thing he remembered with crystalline clarity was watching an al-Adar terrorist with a black kaffiyeh wrapped around his face slit the throat of translator Teresa Miles.

He dreamed about that moment almost every night. The sounds, the smells, the colors and the sensations were as vivid now as they had been three years ago. The quicksilver glint of the knife. The crimson thread bisecting Teresa's long, slender neck. The iron smell of her blood as it flowed from the wound. The pale half-dollar-sized patch of scarred flesh on the wrist of her assassin.

Part of him wanted to believe it was coincidence, that the man who'd killed Teresa hadn't been sitting mere feet away from him today, alive and well and living free.

Another part of him hoped Tahir Mahmoud really was the al-Adar assassin who'd killed Teresa Miles. Because Maddox wanted nothing more in this life than to mete out justice to the bastard his own way.

"Mr. Heller."

Maddox gave a start, sucked out of his black thoughts by the sound of his name. He turned to find Charles Kipler near the front desk, looking uncomfortable in an Italian silk suit the color of a stormy sky.

Maddox took a deep breath, shaking off the ghosts of the past, and pasted on a smile as he crossed to the front desk. "Chuck! Did you know it's ninety degrees outside?" He flicked Kipler's lapel. "You're in the middle of paradise, man, but you look like you're going to a funeral. Lighten up."

"Thank you for the sartorial commentary."

Maddox laughed. "Sartorial commentary? I like that. You're a funny guy, Chuck. Here's a little tip—there's a gift shop just down the hall. I bet they've got a nice 'Mariposa is for Suck-Ups' T-shirt in your size—"

"Actually I'm here to see Iris Browning," Kipler cut him off. "She's not answering her room phone. Have you seen her?"

So Celia Shore and her lackey knew Iris's name now. How had that happened? "Sorry, man. I'm not her social secretary."

"Maddox, I—"

Maddox turned at the sound of Iris's voice. She faltered to a stop, looking from him to Charles Kipler. A little crinkle appeared in her forehead. "I'm sorry. I didn't mean to interrupt."

"No problem. What is it?"

"Miss Browning?" Kipler asked.

Iris's frown deepened. "I'm Iris Browning."

Kipler extended his hand. "Charles Kipler. We spoke on the phone this morning. I'm Celia Shore's manager."

Iris's expression shifted from confusion to tension. It radiated from her like an electrical current, making the hairs on Maddox's arms stand up. She shook Kipler's hand and stepped back, sidling closer to Maddox. "I didn't expect to hear from you so soon. I hope everything's okay with Ms. Shore."

"She's doing very well. In fact, I just brought her here from the hospital. She's in her room resting, but she asked me to find you. She wants to talk to you."

Iris glanced at Maddox. "I'd like to talk to her, as well."

"Good. I'll contact her and see if she's ready. If you'll excuse me." Kipler crossed back to the desk and picked up the courtesy phone.

Iris closed her fingers around Maddox's arm. "What should I ask her?"

He met her desperate gaze with surprise. "I don't know, sugar. What do you think she can tell you?"

She lowered her voice. "I believe she was part of Dr. Grinkov's focus group. If she can remember what happened to her, she may be able to tell me where Sandrine is."

"I don't think she remembers anything."

"Then I'll have to make her remember."

"How're you gonna do that?" He waved his hand in front of her forehead. "You got some kind of special mind rays, you're gonna pull the memories out of her head?" His voice dipped to a growl. "Maybe they taught you something in that seminar, huh?"

She grabbed his hand. "Stop it."

"I don't think she's gonna remember for you." He squeezed her hand. "You know, you don't have to talk to her if you don't want to. I can tell you're nervous about it."

"I have to risk it."

He cocked his head. She really didn't look forward to talking to Celia Shore. He just didn't understand why. "You want me to come with you?"

She shook her head. "No. It's okay. I'll be fine."

He opened his hand, threading his fingers through hers. Her palm was warm and soft against his. "You sure?"

She nodded. "Positive."

He started to let go of her hand, but she tightened her fingers, snaring his palm against hers. "I'm sorry, Maddox."

He frowned, not following. "For what?"

"For what I said back there. About people warning me to stay away from you."

He looked away from her earnest gaze, afraid of what he'd see in her eyes. "Nothing to be sorry for, sugar. It wasn't a lie, was it?"

Her thumb moved lightly over his. "No. But I don't have to listen to what they say."

His heart squeezed. "Maybe you should."

Her fingers tightened. "What if I can't?"

"All set," Charles Kipler interrupted.

Iris released Maddox's hand and turned to Kipler. "When does she want to see me?"

"Right now."

Iris's dark eyes lifted, briefly meeting Maddox's gaze. He sent her silent assurances that she'd be okay.

She looked back at Kipler. "Let's go."

Maddox stood in the center of the lobby and watched her go, his gaze not leaving her back until she rounded the corner toward the elevators. He released a shaky breath, the feel of Iris's hand lingering in the flesh of his palm.

The mess he was in had just gotten a lot messier.

CHARLES KIPLER led Iris to the Hotel St. George's penthouse suite, where she found Celia Shore lounging prettily on a damask silk sofa in the living area. Kipler made the introductions.

"Thank you, Charles," Celia said. "That will be all."

Kipler faded into the next room, leaving them alone.

"Please, sit." Celia waved at the armchair next to the sofa. "May I call you Iris?"

Iris sat. "If you like."

"Good. Call me Celia. Can I get you something to drink?"

"No, thank you."

Celia cocked her head. "You look different than I remember."

"So do you." Iris threaded her fingers together in her lap. "I was surprised to hear you wanted to see me. I can't imagine what for."

"I think you can," Celia said with a cryptic smile. "I wanted to thank you for what you did for me yesterday."

Iris looked down at her twisting hands. "I didn't do anything."

"We both know you did. Don't we?"

Iris forced herself to meet Celia's gaze. The woman's expression was placid and sure. "I don't—"

"You're a healer." Celia leaned toward her, reaching out her hand. She clasped Iris's hand in her cool grip. "I felt it yesterday, when you held my hand. That's what you are, isn't it? You're a healer, like me."

Iris drew her hand away. "I'm not like you."

Celia's eyes narrowed, but she didn't respond.

"You're not a healer," Iris continued, knowing she shouldn't say it aloud. She should smile and pretend that Celia was exactly what she claimed to be. She needed answers from Celia, after all. But sitting beside the woman in this fancy penthouse, seeing the fruits of her lies, was more than Iris could take.

"I don't know what you mean."

"Yes, you do," Iris countered. "You're not a healer. You're just very good at reading people, and you're a good saleswoman. You know where to find a likely mark and what to tell them to make them feel better about themselves. And the camera loves you. You're perfect for what you do, but you're not a healer."

Celia's placid mask cracked a bit, her lower lip beginning to tremble. She looked away from Iris. "That's not a very nice thing to say."

"It's not a very nice thing to do."

"I don't know who you think you are—"

"I'm someone who can do what you say you can." Iris caught Celia's hand and squeezed tightly, opening herself to what the other woman was feeling. A dozen little physical twinges fluttered over her body, mere gnats compared to the monster of fear rampaging through Celia at the moment. "I know your back hurts. You have a large bruise just below your rib cage. And you're terrified of what I'm saying to you right now."

Celia jerked her hand away. "I think you should go."

"Not yet." Iris leaned toward her. "If you could really do what you say you can, you wouldn't advertise. You wouldn't want clients. You sure as hell wouldn't plaster your face across TV or build yourself a big, fancy Web site. Nobody in the world, no matter how good-hearted, would willingly seek out the kind of pain that comes with being a psychic healer."

Silence fell between them. Celia broke it with a shaky breath. "What do you intend to do?"

Iris sat back again. "Why would I do anything? People obviously get something from their sessions with you or they wouldn't come back. Who am I to tell them they're wrong?"

"Then why did you come here? To make me feel bad?"

"No." Iris released a shaky laugh, realizing she'd probably sabotaged any hope of help from Celia.

"You want something from me."

Iris looked at Celia. "You *are* good at reading people."

Celia's eyes narrowed with suspicion. "I never read you as a blackmailer."

Iris tried not to bristle. A woman who practiced deceit was likely to expect it in others. "I'm not. I just want answers."

"About what?"

"You came here for the conference. Are you sure you don't remember anything about arriving here? You spoke at an early seminar."

"I don't remember."

Iris pulled the sheet of paper Sharon had given her from her purse and unfolded it. She read off the list of names. "Are any of those familiar to you?"

"I've heard of a couple of them, but I've never met them."

"Are you sure?"

"I'm sure."

"Maybe you met them here at the conference."

"I told you I don't remember anything since the airport."

"Just try," Iris insisted.

"Don't you think I have been?" Celia's voice rose. "Do you think I like not knowing where I was or what I was doing or what was being done to me during the missing time?"

Iris braced herself against the flood of fear pouring from Celia like sweat. "I'm sorry. I know it's hard for you. But my friend is missing, and I think what happened to you may be important."

"Missing?"

"She was supposed to meet me at the airport day before yesterday. She didn't show." Iris told Celia about her search for her friend, about the frustrations and dead ends. "Your names are both on this list. You were part of a special focus group that Dr. Grinkov culled from the conference. Do you have any memory of that?"

Celia frowned. "No. I'm sorry."

Iris hid her frustration. Whatever her ethics, Celia Shore

seemed genuinely distressed by what was happening to her. Iris didn't want to add to her pain.

She stood. "I'm sorry, too. I don't mean to make things hard for you. I should go now."

Celia grabbed her hand. "Wait. You won't tell anyone, will you?"

"I said I wouldn't."

Celia let go of Iris's hand. "Thank you. If I remember anything that will help you find your friend, I promise you I'll be in touch."

"Thank you." Iris left the penthouse suite and walked slowly toward the elevators, her knees shaking.

She'd so hoped that Celia had answers for her. Maddox had warned her not to expect too much. He'd been right.

Inside the elevator, she slumped against the back of the car and stared at herself in the mirrored walls. She looked tired, pale and fragile. She'd never thought of herself in those terms, but the evidence of her rapid decline stared back at her, impossible to deny.

She should have stayed in Willow Grove, down in her basement laboratory, away from people and problems and pain.

She pressed the button for her room floor, no longer in the mood to attend any of the Cassandra Society's conference seminars. When she stepped out of the elevator, she was surprised to see Maddox sitting in the hall beside her door.

He looked up as she approached. "How'd it go?"

"Fine." She unlocked the hotel room door. "How did you know I'd come here instead of go back to the conference?"

"Maybe I'm psychic." He pushed to his feet and followed her inside. "You don't look like it went fine."

She threw her purse on the bed and turned to face him. "Thanks for constantly reminding me how terrible I look."

His brow wrinkled. "I didn't mean it that way, Iris."

She sank onto the side of the bed, slumping her head to her chest. "You were right. She didn't remember anything."

"I'm sorry." He sat next to her, his shoulder pressed against hers. "I take it you're all seminared out for today?"

She nodded.

"Hungry?"

"Not really."

"You look like you could use a little lunch."

She slanted a look at him. "Again with the compliments."

He took her hand. "Come on, you don't need an old beach bum like me to tell you what a pretty woman you are, do you?"

"Couldn't hurt," she admitted, going for a light tone but missing. Some of her doubts bled through, revealing more than she'd intended.

"You're a pretty woman, Iris Browning." He brought her hand to his lips and kissed her knuckles. His mouth was warm and soft, and the heat that flowed from that light caress chased away some of her despair.

She wanted to ask him why he was being so sweet to her, but she was afraid of the answer. So she gently pulled her hand away from his and stood to put some distance between them, crossing to the window overlooking the balcony and the sea beyond. "I meant to ask you, did you show that sketch of the bearded man around town?"

He didn't answer right away, drawing her gaze back to him. He was looking at a spot on the far wall, his expression hard to read. She couldn't even sense what he was feeling.

"Haven't had a chance," he answered finally. "You were probably right about him, though. He has a missing friend, he said. That's probably all there was to it."

Now he was lying. She didn't have to be an empath to tell.

But why? What was his game? Why would a guy like Maddox spend so much time worrying about her problems?

He wouldn't. Not without his own agenda. She had to quit thinking of him as someone she could afford to get close to.

She pushed her disappointment into a tight little place inside her and turned to look at him. "You know, I think I'd just like to lie down for a while. I'm sure you have better things to do than sit around here holding my hand."

He shot her a now familiar salacious smile. "I don't know, sounds like it could be fun."

She didn't rise to his bait. "I'll see you around, okay?"

His smile faded. "Okay. You call me if you need me." He grabbed a piece of hotel stationery from the desk by the bed and jotted something on it. "That's my cell phone number. I'll leave it on in case you need me."

"Thank you," she said.

But she had no intention of needing Maddox anymore.

She closed the door behind him and leaned against it, her heart racing.

An hour later, the nap she'd planned to take continued to elude her. Maybe she'd been wrong to come back here instead of returning to the conference. What if someone at the seminar could tell her more about Dr. Grinkov's Telaraña lab and just exactly what it was he did there?

She grabbed her purse and headed out the door.

Halfway down the hall, she felt a prickling sensation on the back of her neck. A gnawing emptiness carved a hollow in her belly. She faltered to a stop, recognizing the sensation. Slowly, she turned and looked down the hall behind her.

A few feet away stood the bearded man from the Tropico. Panic knotted her insides. "I'll scream."

He closed the distance between them in a heartbeat, covering her mouth. "No, you won't."

Chapter Eight

"Oh. You again."

Maddox looked up to find Charles Kipler standing in front of him. "Chuck! Fetching lunch for the missus?"

A glint of humor lightened Kipler's eyes, catching Maddox by surprise. "Yeah. You, too?"

Maddox looked down at the take-out ticket in his hand. "She said she wasn't hungry. But she needs to eat."

Kipler sat next to Maddox, flipping his own take-out ticket between his fingers. "Did Ms. Browning tell you what she and Celia spoke about?"

"You don't know?"

"No."

Maddox shook his head. "Me, either."

Kipler loosened his tie. "I thought you didn't know Ms. Browning. Just some tourist, you said."

"She is."

"Rather pretty one."

Maddox slanted a look at him. "Chuck, I think I liked it better when we weren't sittin' around having heart-to-hearts."

The cashier announced the arrival of Maddox's order. He waggled the ticket at Kipler and went to pay for the food.

He probably should have asked Iris if she minded an impromptu lunch date, but he was afraid she'd say no. For a woman who looked like a delicate hothouse flower most of the time, she had a stubborn streak as wide as the Mississippi. She didn't like to be treated as if she were fragile.

He respected that attitude, but he was also afraid that she was pushing herself too hard. She'd gone through a lot in the past two days, trying to help her missing friend. She needed to take some time to take care of herself.

The elevator doors opened on the fourth floor and he exited, balancing the take-out boxes, which were beginning to tilt. With his attention focused on the boxes, he was several steps down the hall before he looked up.

He froze, his mind shifting gears too slowly.

Iris was struggling with the bearded man a few yards away.

Maddox dropped the boxes to the floor and raced toward them, anger bubbling up in his gut. "Quinn!"

Quinn let go of Iris and started running for the stairs. Iris ran to Maddox, flinging herself into his arms. He could feel the triple-time cadence of her heartbeat against his chest.

"It's okay, Iris. I've got you." He cradled her face between his hands. "You okay? He didn't hurt you?"

"I'm okay." She let go of him and stepped back, taking a couple of long, trembling breaths.

"Did he say anything to you?"

She shook her head. "Just to be quiet and go into my room with him. I couldn't let him get me in there."

Maddox gazed past her toward the stairway exit, his eyes

narrowed. "Iris, lock yourself in your room. Don't let anyone in but me." He released her and started toward the stairs.

"What are you doing?"

"Just lock yourself in your room!" He raced for the stairs, easing the door open and stepping inside the stairwell. He paused at the top landing, listening for sounds.

Quinn would expect him to follow. The obvious choice would be to head down the stairs toward an exit.

But Quinn was anything but obvious.

What was his game? Obviously he wanted something from Iris—was it connected to the conference? If Maddox was right about Tahir Mahmoud, Quinn would definitely want to know why an al-Adar terrorist with a lot of innocent American blood on his hands was attending a psychics' conference in Mariposa.

But what did that have to do with Iris? Why her?

Maddox started up the steps to the next floor. He turned at the landing and faltered to a stop.

Quinn stood at the top of the stairs, leaning against the wall. "I was wondering if you'd drag yourself away from her long enough to follow."

"What do you want from her?"

"You know I can't tell you that."

"You think I'd burn you?" Maddox glared at him. "Man, you don't know me at all."

"I think you'd keep her from doing what I need her to do." Quinn started down the steps toward him.

"I won't let you hurt her."

"I don't intend to hurt her."

"You never do."

Quinn's hazel eyes hardened. "Don't get in my way."

Maddox blocked him from passing. "Or what?"

Quinn launched himself from the third step, slamming Maddox backward into the wall of the stairwell. His head hit the concrete block wall with a crack, blackening his vision for a second. Quinn followed his advantage with two quick, hammerlike jabs to Maddox's gut, knocking the wind out of him.

Quinn grabbed his arm and whirled him around, slamming him face-first into the wall. Maddox's knee twisted, hot agony sparking up his leg to join the symphony of pain.

Gritting his teeth, Maddox focused on the sound of Quinn's rapid breathing, trying to anticipate the next blow. The second he felt it coming, he threw back his head, his skull connecting with Quinn's face. A grunt escaped Quinn's throat.

Maddox whirled around, ignoring the throbbing in his knee, and drove his body into Quinn's, hurling them both against the stairs. He landed a couple of punches to Quinn's gut and jaw before Quinn lashed out with a vicious kick that caught him in the groin. Pain exploded in his pelvis and rocketed up his gut, sending nausea coursing through him. He dropped to his knees, the ache in his twisted knee racing up his leg.

He managed to lift his head and found himself staring down the barrel of a 9 mm Beretta.

"You can't win this." Quinn wiped blood from his battered nose and steadied the Beretta.

Maddox glared at him, trying to catch his breath.

"I want you to go home and forget you ever met a woman named Iris Browning. Do you understand?"

Maddox's profane response made Quinn's lips curve.

"I was afraid you'd be that way," Quinn said. He put the Beretta's barrel against Maddox's forehead. "Turn around and face the wall. Stay on your knees."

Maddox did what Quinn told him, his heart racing. "You're not going to kill me."

"Why would I kill you?" Quinn asked.

Then Maddox's world exploded into blackness.

IRIS WATCHED the hands of her travel alarm clock click forward another minute. Twelve-fifteen. Maddox had been gone almost ten minutes.

Where was he? Was he okay?

The hotel room doorknob rattled softly, drawing her gaze to the door. She heard the soft snick of the lock disengage. Her heart pounding, she looked at the safety latch at the top of the door. She hadn't engaged it, she realized, panic icing her insides.

She pushed to her feet, her legs slow and uncooperative. She couldn't draw a deep breath, her brain turning to sludge as she tried to figure out what to do, where she could hide.

The balcony. She scrambled over the bed and raced for the glass doors to the balcony.

"Stay where you are." The gravelly voice of the bearded man sliced through the haze of fear, drawing her to a halt.

She turned slowly to face him, what was left of her breath escaping in a soft gasp. He was disheveled, his shirt torn at the shoulder and blood streaking his nose and chin. Obviously, he'd been in a fight. And if he'd come out the winner—

"What did you do to Maddox?" she asked, her voice raspy with fear.

"He'll live." He spoke with a flat, neutral American accent now, all traces of his earlier clipped tones gone.

"What do you want with me?"

The bearded man turned and started to close the door behind him. But it flew open, knocking him backward into the dresser.

Maddox stumbled into the room, bruises and scrapes covering his face and arms. He lurched at the bearded man, grabbing the man by both arms and hauling him face-first down onto the bed.

Iris backed up against the balcony doors, her pulse loud and fast in her head. Pain zigzagged through her, setting off little knots of agony all over her body. Her head. Her nose. Her knee. Her stomach and groin. Both men had taken a beating, and she could feel every bit of it.

"Maddox—" she gasped.

He glanced at her, looking quickly back at the bearded man who had started to squirm beneath his grasp. Maddox pulled something out of the back of the man's trousers and shoved it against the back of the man's head.

A gun, Iris realized, panic setting in all over again. "Maddox, don't—"

Maddox looked up at her, his eyes cold and hard. His breathing was fast and labored, his jaw tight with anger. Iris could feel his fear, his rage, so overwhelming that it blotted out all the twinges and pains from both men's injuries.

He jerked the bearded man to his feet. "Give me the key."

The man reached into the pocket of his trousers.

"Slowly," Maddox warned with a growl.

The bearded man withdrew a room key and handed it to Maddox. "You don't know what you're doing."

"Yes, I do." He grabbed the man and shoved him up against the wall by the door. He kept the gun barrel tight against the base of the man's skull as he jerked open the door. With a hard shove, he sent the intruder through the door into the corridor. "Don't come back."

The stranger turned to face Maddox, his green glare as hard as stone. "It's not over, Heller."

Maddox slammed the door in his face and engaged the safety bolt. He turned to face Iris, wiping blood from his cheek with the back of his arm. "You okay?"

She nodded. "I'm fine."

He laid the Beretta on the dresser and walked slowly to where she stood by the balcony doors, his steps unsteady.

"I was so afraid," she whispered, stepping toward him as he closed the space between them. "I was so afraid of what he'd done to you—"

He cradled her face between his hands. "You don't have to be afraid. It's okay."

She touched his cheek, a soft hiss escaping her lips. "You're hurt."

His gaze settled on her lips. "No, I'm fine," he murmured, dipping his head toward her.

She should push him away. The aches and twinges rolling off of his battered body were almost more than she could bear, and he'd barely touched her yet. But a different sort of ache had settled over her the second he took a step toward her. A need to be closer to him, to feel his skin on hers.

His mouth moved over hers, gentle but hungry. Her lips parted, her breath mingling with his. He released a low groan of pleasure that rumbled like thunder around them.

"Iris," he whispered against her lips, his hands sliding up her back, bunching the soft jersey cotton of her sundress under his palms.

She felt every pain he was feeling, but she also felt the heat of his desire, a flame racing to meet the blaze of her own need where it simmered low in her belly. The potent mingling of pain and pleasure came as a surprise; she hadn't known until this moment that they were two sides of the same coin.

She threaded her fingers through his hair, curling, twining, pulling him closer. His tongue darted against hers in response, an invitation she couldn't have refused if she'd wanted to. He started backing toward the bed, bringing her with him. She went willingly, wanting more. Wanting everything.

His knees buckled as he hit the edge of the bed, and he fell backward, pulling her down on top of him. His knee twisted as they went down. Agony wrenched through her leg, making her gasp. She forced her mind back to the pleasure of his hands on her back, large and strong, holding her to him.

When he pushed her away suddenly, she almost fell off the bed. She caught herself, rising to a sitting position next to him. She scraped her hair out of her eyes and stared at him, confused. "Maddox?"

He turned to look at her, his blue eyes dark and fierce beneath his furrowed brow. "You felt that," he said.

IRIS MET his gaze with pain-dark eyes. She didn't answer him, just stared at him with a curious mixture of fear and hope.

Nausea shuddered through his gut. He swallowed hard, forcing it away. "It's what that woman talked about at the lecture. What do you call it—empathic sensitivity. Right?"

Even as he said the words, he knew they were crazy. Empathic sensitivity? What the hell was that? Who the hell believed in such a thing?

That blow to the head must've been worse than he'd thought.

Iris started crying. It wasn't the way he'd seen her cry before, softly and quietly. It was a floodgate opening, racking her with sobs. She bent forward, burying her face in her hands, and cried like a brokenhearted child.

He sat against the pillows and watched her, afraid to touch her for fear that somehow his crazy idea was right. It would explain everything that had puzzled him about her, wouldn't it? How she knew what Celia Shore's injuries were. Why she seemed to be in constant pain— was she picking up on the aches and pains of all the people around her?

He shook his head, closing his eyes to the sight of her anguish. The idea was nuts. *He* was nuts to even consider it.

Yet somehow she'd reacted to his pain as surely as he had. When his knee had twisted as they fell to the bed, she'd gasped before he'd even really felt the pain.

She'd felt it.

Her sobs subsided to a weak hitching noise. He forced himself to open his eyes and look at her. She lifted her chin and met his gaze, her lips still trembling. "I should call the hotel doctor."

He shook his head. "I don't need a doctor." He didn't want to bring a doctor into this mess. If he saw a doctor, the cops would eventually show up. He didn't have much use for Mariposa's finest on a good day.

"Of course you need a doctor."

"Iris, talk to me. You just felt—"

"You need to lie down. You're hurt." She pushed away from the bed, wobbling a little, and took his arm. "Lie down and let me take a look at your injuries."

He looked at her through narrowed eyes, confused and suddenly scared as hell. "I thought you were a botanist, not a nurse."

"Shut up and quit fighting me."

He forced a pained chuckle. "Forceful. I like that." He stopped resisting, allowing himself the painful luxury of inhaling the fresh soap-and-water smell of her as she helped him lie back on the bed. She was warm where she touched him.

He sank against the pillows, trying not to breathe too deeply. Now that lust and adrenaline had both begun draining away, he was feeling the full force of his injuries. He hoped the stabbing pain in his rib cage was just a bruise and not something worse.

Iris suddenly sat down on the bed, wrapping her arms around her middle and doubling over. A quiet whimper escaped her lips.

Maddox sat forward, closing his fingers around her wrist. She winced and pulled her arm away.

He leaned back against the headboard, his heart racing. "I'm right, aren't I? You do feel that."

Slowly, she turned and laid her hand on his left shin. She couldn't hold back a grimace of pain. She took a deep breath and spoke. "Your ribs are bruised on the left side. One may be cracked—I'm not sure of that. You twisted your knee at some point. It's aching. When you got hit on your jaw, it scraped the inside of your cheek against your teeth. It's raw and probably bleeding."

He ran his tongue along the inside of his mouth. The flesh was torn and tender.

"You got hurt…somewhere else, too." Her gaze dropped to the zipper of his jeans.

Laughing to keep from freaking out, he bent forward, his ribs screaming in painful protest, and pushed her hand off his leg. "Don't touch me, Iris."

The stricken look she gave him made his stomach hurt. She pushed herself off the end of the bed and retreated to the window, her back to him. Her shoulders shook with new tears.

"I'm sorry," he said. "I just don't want you to have to feel what I'm feeling right now."

She turned to look at him. Daylight filtering through the window outlined her with gold, obscuring her features so that he couldn't read her expression as she slowly approached the bed.

She stopped beside him. "I can do more than feel it."

He frowned at her, not understanding.

She sat on the bed beside him and twined her fingers with his. Her forehead crinkled with pain.

Then he felt it. Electric prickling, like a numb limb coming to life, a release of energy from his body to hers. Agony swirled out of him as if she'd pulled the stopper on a drain. Her face went ashen, but her grip on his hand tightened, as if that connection were all that was holding her upright.

He jerked his hand out of hers, and she whimpered.

"Stop it!" he growled, shifting into a sitting position.

He had to get out of here.

"Let me finish," she whispered, reaching for him again.

He gently pushed her hands away. "No."

She closed her eyes, her chin dropping to her chest. She was breathing hard, as if she'd just run a race.

"This is why you fell down in the street yesterday," he said past the lump in his throat as he watched tears spill down her cheeks. "It's what you were doing at the beach when you held Celia's hand. That's why she wanted to see you, isn't it? Because she felt what you could do."

Her voice cracked. "You think I'm a freak."

He didn't know how to answer. It was just so—impossible.

She stood up, swaying slightly, her slender body like a reed in the wind. "It's okay. You're not the first."

His heart twisted as if hands had reached into his chest and wrung it dry. He tamped down the feeling, hiding the pain from himself. From her.

He let silence fall between them, as heavy as the dread settling over him as he watched her cry. For several minutes, only the harsh sound of his own breathing and the damp whisper of her tears intruded on the quiet. Then, slowly another sound filtered into his consciousness.

Sirens.

Chapter Nine

Maddox turned to Iris, dread sitting heavy on his chest. "Did you call the cops?"

She looked at him, wide-eyed. "No."

Maybe the cops were just passing by, he thought, trying to ignore the voice inside him warning him trouble was on the way.

Iris crossed to the balcony, holding on to the door frame to keep her balance. She peered out at the beach road beyond. "They're coming here. Maybe someone reported your fight."

He pushed himself off the bed, blackness rimming his vision as agony unleashed itself on his injured ribs. He groped for the wall, taking care not to touch Iris. He spotted a couple of Mariposa police cruisers, as well as a fire truck and an emergency ambulance. "Maybe an accident or something."

"What if that guy was hurt worse than he looked?" Iris glanced over her shoulder at him. "Maybe he passed out."

"Listen, you stay right here. Okay? I've gotta go get something." He'd left the food boxes out in the hall. If the police came through this section of the hotel and spotted them, they might be curious enough to start knocking on all the doors.

He went down the hall and picked up the boxes. They were wrapped in clear plastic sheeting, which had kept them from spilling their contents when he dropped them to the carpet. The food was probably a mishmash now, but he didn't think either of them was hungry anymore.

He knocked on Iris's door. "Me again."

She let him in. "What's in the boxes?"

He managed a pained grin. "I was feeling a little hungry."

"Two lunches' worth of hungry?"

He smiled at her skeptical tone. "I thought I might find a pretty tourist to share a little chow with me. Know anybody like that?"

She managed a half smile. "Sorry, no."

He flashed her a wicked grin. "Come on. Sure you do."

Her smile faded and she stepped back.

He stepped toward her, regretting his words. When was he going to learn to shut his mouth? "Iris?"

"Quinn," she said. "That man—you called him Quinn. And he knew your name, too."

He sighed. So she'd heard that.

She stared at him. "You know him, don't you?"

He hesitated, well aware that he couldn't tell her who Quinn really was. But he didn't like lying, either. "Sort of."

"Who is he?"

He debated a couple of lies but finally opted for the truth. "I can't tell you that."

Her brow wrinkled. "What do you mean, you can't tell me?"

"I can't explain. I'm sorry."

"That's insane! That man just broke into my room and beat you up, and you can't tell me who he is?" Her gaze darkened. "Who are you protecting?"

A knock on the door interrupted. They both turned and stared at the closed door.

"Who is it?" Iris asked.

"Mariposa police."

Damn it. Maddox looked at the gun lying on the dresser. He actually had an island gun permit, but not for that Beretta. He pushed himself to the dresser and put the Beretta in the middle drawer, tucking it under a filmy pair of silk panties. "I'll wash up," he told Iris, heading into the bathroom.

He ran water and grabbed a washcloth, wincing as the wet, rough terry cloth scraped across the abrasion on his cheek. He didn't seem to be bleeding anywhere else, but his whole body felt as if he'd been trampled by elephants.

Quinn shouldn't have been able to get the first punch in. He'd lost his edge over the past three years.

He heard the low murmur of voices outside but couldn't make out any words. He laid the washcloth on the sink and opened the bathroom door, bracing himself for whatever came next.

A pair of detectives in street clothes sat in matching chairs at the small table near the balcony. Maddox recognized the taller of the two—Melvin Lively, a round-faced Mariposan with a ready grin and an extensive vocabulary of profanities he used with abandon whenever he was losing at pool. Which was often. He gave Maddox a small nod of recognition.

Iris sat on the bed, her back ruler-straight. Her dark eyes met his. "Celia's dead."

Maddox's knees buckled for a second. He caught himself on the edge of the dresser. "What? How?"

Iris looked at the two policemen. They remained silent. "Mr. Kipler gave the police my name."

Maddox sat next to her on the bed, glaring at Lively. "You're not suggesting—"

"No, we're certain Ms. Shore was killed by someone rather larger than she was. Which Ms. Browning is not."

Left unsaid, however, was the fact that Maddox *was* larger than Celia. The hint of accusation lingered in the brief silence, adding to Maddox's growing sense of dread. "How was she killed?"

"We're trying to establish a timeline." The shorter of the two detectives ignored the question. He was European in background, his local accent slightly tinged with the clipped cadence of the Dutch. "Ms. Browning says that she was with you from the time she left Ms. Shore's room, except for a few minutes while you were downstairs getting lunch."

Maddox looked at the two unopened boxes. "That's right."

"Can you verify your whereabouts from the time you left Ms. Browning's hotel room until you returned?"

"The cashier at the restaurant would've seen me," he answered automatically. "I talked to Charles Kipler there, as well. I think he was getting dinner for Celia."

His mind rebelled at the thought of Celia Shore being dead. It wasn't as if he hadn't seen death before. God knew, he had. But she'd been okay the last time he saw her. Getting better. Who would hate her enough to kill her?

"Did you and Mr. Kipler have a fight?" Melvin Lively asked.

Maddox lifted his hand to his scraped cheek. "No. Fell down some stairs."

He felt Iris's gaze on him. He cut his eyes toward her, hoping she'd follow his lead. The cops didn't need to know about Quinn's visit. That was something he was going to have to handle on his own, quietly.

"Are you sure?" the shorter detective asked.

"Positive. I was just about to let Ms. Browning play doctor with me." He shot her an exaggerated leer. Her look in return was about as queasy as he felt.

"You'll understand if we defer that 'til later," Lively said, his dark eyes amused despite the serious look on his face.

Maddox's smile faded. "Yeah, I understand."

"Good. Now, can we go over this one more time?"

IRIS COULD ADD little to the detective's knowledge of what had happened to Celia Shore. She glanced at Maddox, wondering why she was keeping quiet about the bearded man. Because Maddox wanted her to? Had she lost her mind? What if Quinn had killed Celia? The timing didn't seem right—he'd been here on this floor, trying to get her to let him come into her room, during the short span of time when Celia seemed to have met her end. But was his presence here really a coincidence?

She should say something to the police. Now.

"Doesn't the hotel have surveillance cameras?" Maddox asked, his face pale beneath his tan.

"Someone tampered with them," Melvin said before

the shorter detective could shush him. "Ms. Browning, if you could tell us again about your discussion with Ms. Shore—"

"She already answered that twice, Melvin," Maddox interjected, impatience bleeding from his gritty drawl.

Detective Lively shot Maddox an exasperated look. "You are still here because I'm a nice guy, Mr. Heller. You do not want to make me become a not-so-nice guy."

Maddox's lips thinned to a tight line, but he kept quiet.

Iris answered the detective's question again, glancing at Maddox. She took a deep breath, preparing to bring up the subject of the bearded man who'd accosted her, but the dark look in Maddox's eyes kept her silent.

Okay, she thought. *I'll play it your way. But you're going to tell me who Quinn is and what's going on.*

And if she didn't like his answer, she'd be on the phone to the police before he could turn around twice.

Detective Lively had almost finished taking her through what information she had about Sandrine's disappearance for a second time when a newcomer arrived, a tall, dark-haired man with brown eyes and a lanky build. As the policeman at her door let him in, the man's gaze moved first to Maddox. One dark eyebrow quirked at the sight of his battered face.

The two had met before, Iris realized.

The dark-haired man looked away from Maddox and nodded a greeting to Detective Lively. He spoke with a British accent. "I'll wait outside until you finish, Detective Lively. I don't want to interfere in your investigation—"

"We're wrapping things up, Mr. Darcy," Detective Lively assured him. He stood and closed his notebook.

The man named Darcy stepped closer to Iris. "Miss Browning, I'm Nicholas Darcy with the U.S. consulate. I wanted to leave my contact information and let you know we will be available to help you with any legal issues that may arise from this incident," Darcy said.

"Darcy's the Regional Security Officer—an embassy cop, I guess you'd say." Maddox's voice was inflection-free, but a wave of bitterness flowed into Iris from his direction.

"I'm sorry to hear of Miss Shore's demise. Were you close?" Though he directed the question at Iris, Nicholas Darcy shot Maddox a tight glare.

Maddox returned the look, his jaw squared.

Interesting, Iris thought.

Detective Lively paused in the doorway, bowing slightly toward her. "Ms. Browning, will you be remaining here at the hotel for the next couple of days?"

As Iris opened her mouth to assure the detective she would, Maddox said, "No, she will not."

Iris glared at Maddox. "I beg your pardon?"

Maddox returned the look, his expression deadly serious. Anxiety radiated from him in almost tangible ripples. "A woman was just murdered here. You yourself said you think she may have been part of the same focus group your friend was part of. And you've been asking a lot of questions about that focus group. Why on God's green earth would you stay here in this hotel another minute?" He turned to Nicholas Darcy. "Darcy, there's got to be someplace at the consulate she can stay."

"She's not a refugee, and she's not under any sort of direct threat," Darcy replied in clipped, formal tones, although Iris could feel his ambivalence. The RSO's voice dropped a half tone as he met Maddox's hard gaze. "You know there's nothing I can do under the current circumstances."

Why didn't Maddox tell him about the bearded man? Surely if Mr. Darcy knew about the break-in—

She looked at Maddox. He met her gaze, his eyes narrowed.

"There will be a heavy police presence here for the next day or two," Detective Lively interjected.

"Or you could provide her with protection yourself," Darcy said, still looking at Maddox.

Silence settled over the room in the aftermath of Darcy's quiet suggestion. Iris's stomach knotted, an unexpected gush of sheer terror flooding her chest, interfering with her breathing.

The emotion came from Maddox. When he spoke, his voice was soft and strangled. Fear suffused him, darkened his eyes and dug furrows into his brow and cheeks. "I can't do that."

Iris tried to make sense of what she was feeling. The thought of playing bodyguard to her obviously scared the hell out of him. But why? Because of what she'd revealed to him about her gift this afternoon? Did he find her so scary?

"I could arrange for you to take a room in another hotel," Darcy said, breaking the silence.

"Or I could just stay here," Iris said firmly.

The emotion coming from Maddox shifted. The fear was still there, along with a hot, tight pain in the center of her belly. But she also felt a strange sense of desperation, a jittery edginess that sparked through her limbs.

Maddox turned to look at Detective Lively. "I'll give you my phone number. You can reach her there for the next day or so." He stood and looked at Iris, shooting her a flash of the dimples. "Sorry, danger monkey, I know you liked wrapping your legs around the Harley yesterday, but I drove the Jeep today. I'll go bring it around to the front. You start packing."

This was insane, Iris thought. "I'm not coming with you."

"Yes, you are." Maddox followed the detective out of the hotel room, leaving Iris staring at the empty doorway.

She looked at Nicholas Darcy, wondering why he hadn't intervened. "This is crazy."

He sighed. "Yes, it is."

"The hotel will be perfectly safe." Unfortunately, her declaration didn't sound convincing, even to her own ears. The truth was, she didn't want to stay here another night alone. She wanted to hop the next plane back to the States.

But Sandrine was still missing, and nobody seemed concerned about it but her.

"Heller seems very certain that the hotel is not a safe place for you." Darcy looked concerned.

She frowned at him. He sounded as if he were trying to talk her into going with Maddox. "You can't be suggesting that I go stay with a stranger rather than stay here at a hotel teeming with policemen."

"I didn't realize you considered him a stranger."

"We just met yesterday."

Darcy didn't respond, but the look in his eyes was clear. A lot could happen in a day between a man and a woman.

She looked down, knowing he was right. "Do you think I should go with him?"

"It's not a decision I can make for you," Darcy said.

"You're with the American consulate. I thought you were supposed to protect American citizens abroad."

"Technically, I protect the consulate and its personnel."

"So I'm on my own."

"If you're uncomfortable accepting Heller's offer—"

"It sounded more like an order than an offer."

He smiled at that. "I'll be the first to agree that Maddox Heller is an unmitigated pain in the ass. But he does have experience working security. You could do much worse were you to hire a local bodyguard."

"You're saying he's trustworthy?"

Darcy's smile faded. "I'm saying that he may be the best option available on the island if you truly feel the need to have someone watching out for your safety."

It wasn't exactly a glowing recommendation, but he didn't seem to think Maddox posed any threat to her. Apparently, neither did she, considering how easily she'd given in to his earth-shattering kiss. Heat rose in her cheeks at the memory.

She tamped down the memory of his body against hers, the warm island spice smell of him filling her lungs, the taste of him on her tongue. If she was going to spend the next couple of days with Maddox Heller, the last thing she needed to do was dwell on that kiss.

MADDOX SAT in his Jeep and stared at the revolving red light on the fire truck in the hotel's emergency lane, his heart in his throat.

What the hell was Darcy thinking, suggesting that he take

Iris Browning to his home to protect her? Darcy, of all people, should know just how unfit he was to guard anything more vulnerable than a building or a parking lot. If he screwed that up, what was lost? A car? A big-screen TV?

If he screwed up protecting Iris Browning, she could end up as dead as Celia Shore.

Or Teresa Miles.

He rubbed his gritty eyes with the heels of his palms, taking slow, deep breaths to ward off his rising panic. He was tempted to put the Jeep in gear and drive as far from here as possible. Let Darcy figure out what to do with Iris. Surely the RSO wouldn't just leave her there undefended.

But Darcy wouldn't have a choice. Babysitting pretty American tourists wasn't part of the man's job description. His duty was to protect the consulate. He'd have to go back there sooner or later.

And Iris would be alone and vulnerable again.

Buck up, Maddox. You stuck your nose in her business. That makes her your responsibility.

He forced himself out of the vehicle, his heart pounding.

You've saved lives before, he reminded himself.

But he'd lost lives, as well.

THE RIDE from the Hotel St. George into the thickening rain forest at the center of the island passed in relative silence. Iris told herself she was glad for it. The quiet of the Jeep's interior, broken only by the steady rumble of its motor and the splatter of approaching rain, soothed away some of the lingering pain from her eventful day.

The darkness emanating from Maddox remained, along

with the occasional twinges of pain coming from his battered body, but both sensations had quieted to a dull throbbing buried somewhere deep inside her. She was glad that he was under control enough that she could put off asking any questions until the morning.

Right now, she just wanted to crawl into bed, pull the covers over her head and sleep for a week.

"Home, sweet home," Maddox murmured a few minutes later, pulling her back from the edge of light doze. The Jeep slowed to a stop, and he turned off the engine. She peered through the sheets of rain at the single-story bungalow nestled amid a riot of palms, bougainvillea and a dozen other trees and vines she didn't immediately recognize.

She didn't know that much about real estate in Mariposa, but she knew it couldn't be cheap. Even this far from the beach, the rent or mortgage payment for a home could be prohibitive. She'd expected him to take her to some shabby, characterless apartment complex on the edge of town.

"Nice house," she murmured as he opened the driver's door.

His lips curved but he didn't respond to her comment. Instead, he got out of the Jeep and came around to her side of the vehicle to open the door for her, limping a bit. He handed her an umbrella he pulled from behind the seat. "Watch your step—the yard is a little uneven."

She felt the damp ground drop beneath her feet before he'd gotten the words out of his mouth. His hand shot out, catching her elbow to keep her from stumbling.

He let go quickly as she gasped at the sudden rush of

pain his touch created. His knee was killing him, and the rest of his injuries were joining in the mayhem.

"Let me get your bags," he said.

She started to protest, but he gritted his teeth and ignored her, hauling her two suitcases from the trunk and nodding for her to walk ahead of him to the house.

He labored up the steps behind her, a soft groan escaping his lips as he reached the concrete landing of the narrow front stoop. He unlocked his front door and flicked on a light. "Make yourself comfortable."

The front door led directly into an airy central room. She could see all the way to the back, where a trio of French doors lined the entire wall. Beyond, there was mostly darkness, but she'd caught a glimpse of Mount Stanley behind the house as they'd arrived. He must have an incredible view from those doors.

A leather sofa and a pair of matching armchairs faced each other across a low teak coffee table. A couple of books lay on the table—paperbacks, not pricey picture books. Iris picked up the top one. *Black Hawk Down,* by Mark Bowden. The one beneath was a Stephen King novel.

Peppy reading, she thought, laying the book down.

Maddox crossed to a door in the wall to her left. "The bedroom's in here. There's a bathroom in there, too, so you can shower when you want."

"I don't want to take your bed," she protested. "The couch looks comfortable."

"It is. I sleep there most nights anyway." He opened the bedroom door and slid her bags inside. "The kitchen's there." He waved to his right, where a half wall separated the kitchen from the main room. "Not that much in the fridge, but you can probably find some frozen dinners or something."

"What will you do for a bathroom?"

"There's a half bath off the kitchen." He gestured toward the open bedroom door. "Go on and lie down, Iris. You look tired. I'll just lock up." He crossed the room to check the locks on the French doors.

Iris watched him a moment, trepidation squeezing her heart. What was she thinking, agreeing to this? No matter how familiar Maddox Heller might seem, he was still a stranger to her. She was insane to have come here with him. He was insane to have suggested it.

But it was done. And she was exhausted. There was a bed waiting behind that half-opened door where her bags sat.

She entered the bedroom, tugging her bags out of the doorway so she could close the door. It latched with a click, plunging her into rainy afternoon gloom.

She stood there a moment, swallowed by gray, her rapid breathing the only sound in the void. "What am I doing here?" she asked the silence.

"Good question," a whispery voice replied, just before a hand clapped over her mouth.

Chapter Ten

Maddox checked the locks on the French doors. He didn't normally lock up; his house was secluded from his nearest neighbors, and he had little anyone would want to take.

He'd gotten lax since leaving his former life behind. Now he had to relearn everything he'd forgotten—and fast.

He sat on the sofa and closed his eyes, listening to the sounds of the rain forest. Insects singing in the jungle beyond the French doors. The whisper of the ceiling fan as it stirred the humid air. Rain tapping on the glass panes of the doors and windows. The pounding cadence of his heart.

A soft thud from behind the closed bedroom door jerked him to attention. His eyes snapping open, he crossed to the closed door and listened. There was another faint thump, then silence.

"Iris?"

A flutter of movement filtered from the other side of the door. He heard a muffled whimper, his heart rate doubling. He turned the doorknob. It rattled uselessly in his hand. Locked.

A loud crash jolted his nerves. He drew the Beretta he'd retrieved from the hotel dresser before he and Iris had left, stepped back and kicked at the door, splintering the wood. Three kicks later, the door broke open to reveal two shadowy figures struggling in the darkened bedroom. Leveling the Beretta, Maddox flicked on the light.

The shadows froze, two sets of eyes turning toward him. Iris's gaze widened, and she slammed her head back, smashing the mouth of her captor, taking advantage of his distraction.

Letting out a string of curses, Quinn loosened his grip, and Iris jerked free, dashing to Maddox's side.

He grabbed her arm and pulled her behind him. "Go into the living room, Iris."

Her fingers closed around his arm. "What's he doing here?"

Quinn wiped his bloody lip with the back of his hand, his gaze never wavering from Maddox's. A glint of humor lightened his hazel eyes. "Did you teach her that move, Heller?"

Rage burned a hole in Maddox's gut. He forced it back, struggling for control. "What the hell are you doing, Quinn?"

"Quinn who?" Iris's voice was still close behind him.

"I told you to go to the living room, Iris."

"You didn't tell her?" Alexander Quinn took a step forward, looking surprised.

Maddox twitched the gun. "I didn't say you could move."

Quinn halted in the middle of the bedroom.

"Somebody tell me what's going on—now," Iris demanded.

Quinn arched an eyebrow at Maddox. "Go ahead, Maddox. Tell her who I am. Tell her how you know me."

A muscle knotted in Maddox's jaw. He took a deep breath to keep from launching himself at Quinn. "Go to hell."

"Fine," Iris said. "The Mariposa police can sort it out."

"I wouldn't do that," Quinn said.

"Well, I'm not you," Iris said, stepping forward to stand next to Maddox. "And you have a gun pointed at your heart. So I get to call the shots here."

"Actually, Heller has the gun. He gets to call the shots," Quinn corrected, looking back at Maddox. "What's it going to be, Heller? In the mood for an international incident?"

Maddox gritted his teeth and slowly lowered the gun.

"What are you doing?" Iris asked, her voice trembling.

Maddox tucked the gun behind his back and caught her arm as she started for the door. "Just calm down—"

She jerked her arm away from him. "I trusted you!"

"You don't understand—"

She looked from him to Quinn and back. The look of betrayal on her face made his stomach ache. "You're in on it."

"Tell her who I am, Maddox."

Maddox shot a look at Quinn. "Are you sure?"

Quinn nodded. "I was going to tell her myself, but she kept fighting back. I wasn't expecting that."

"Who are you?" Iris asked. She looked at Maddox, lowering her voice. "For that matter, who are *you?*"

Maddox laughed, the absurdity of the situation hitting him like a body blow. A day ago, his only worry was whether he had enough spending money to get by another week without dipping into the trust fund. Now here he was, standing in the wrecked remains of his bedroom between a pretty tourist and a man he'd hoped he'd never see again.

"I'm just a beach bum, sugar." Mirthless laughter lingered in his voice. "What you see is what you get. But him?" He gestured at Quinn. "That's Alexander Quinn of the CIA."

Iris released a soft hiss of surprise. "CIA?"

"Central Intelligence Agency," Quinn offered helpfully.

Iris rounded on him, her eyes flashing with fury. "I know what CIA stands for."

Quinn glanced at Maddox. "Beach bum?"

Maddox didn't answer, shooting him a warning look.

Iris crossed the bedroom, stopping a couple of feet out of Quinn's reach. "What does the CIA want with me?"

"I'd like to know that myself," Maddox murmured.

Iris turned around slowly, a look of hurt spreading over her face. "Why didn't you tell me who he was?"

"I couldn't." He knew it probably sounded like a lame excuse to her. But he'd learned a long time ago that loose lips didn't just sink ships, they got people killed.

He wasn't going to be the guy to burn a CIA agent.

Understanding flickered in Iris's eyes. "You couldn't blow his cover. Of course you couldn't tell me. It's like treason."

"Why don't we go in there and talk—" Quinn began.

Maddox glared at him. "Why don't you start explaining why you broke in here and what you want from us?"

"I don't want anything from you." Quinn met Maddox's gaze with a cold stare of his own. "It's her help I need."

"SHE'S NOT going to play spy for you," Maddox said.

"I think that's up to Ms. Browning."

"For God's sake, call me Iris," she interjected. She was exhausted, she was afraid, and she was tired of being buffeted like a beach ball between the iron wills of the two men sitting across from her. "You probably already know my bra size and the results of my latest dental exam, anyway."

"A cavity in your left bicuspid and a molar that needs watching," Quinn murmured with a half smile.

Iris felt a spark of humor breaking through the emptiness coming from him, like a bubble popping in her chest. "Funny."

"I need you. You have access and a strong motive to help me get inside the Cassandra Society's focus group." Quinn pinned her with a gaze so intense, it felt like a sledgehammer slamming into her body. "You want to find Sandrine Beck. I want to know if Dr. Grinkov's experiment is a cover for terrorist activity. We can both get what we want."

"How could a hoodoo convention be a cover for terrorists?" Maddox's question drew Iris's attention to him. He had asked the question of Quinn, but his gaze was fixed on her face.

"It's not exactly unheard of for intelligence agencies to experiment with parapsychology," Quinn answered.

"Remote viewing experiments," Iris murmured, turning her gaze to the CIA agent. "I thought that was a myth."

"We're not talking about governments here," Maddox argued. "Since when did terrorists get into the hoodoo business?"

"That's part of what I want Iris to find out."

Iris felt a surge of dark energy flow from Maddox. He stood suddenly and started pacing toward the window. "You know what she can do, don't you?" he asked Quinn.

Iris looked at Maddox, her emotions trapped somewhere between bemusement and dismay. "Of course he does."

Maddox returned to the sofa. "This is crazy."

She took a deep breath, trying not to be hurt by his words. It was a lot to process, and he'd already had a hellish day.

She looked at Quinn. "I need time to think about it, Mr. Quinn. I'm exhausted. I need sleep. Please, can we discuss this another time?"

Maddox stood. "That's it. Quinn, get out of here."

Quinn rose unhurriedly from his seat. He moved to Iris's side and touched her shoulder. A jolt of pure, hot terror coursed into her from the point of contact. She gazed up at him, trying to make sense of what she was feeling.

Then she realized it wasn't a real emotion. It was manufactured, built from thoughts and memories and suppositions pouring from the CIA agent's darkened soul. He wanted her to know what terror felt like.

He wanted her to know what was at stake.

"Think hard about it, Iris." He released her shoulder.

She slumped against the sofa, shaking.

"That's enough." Maddox grabbed Quinn and shoved him across the room to the front door. He jerked open the door and pushed the agent through. "Get the hell out of my house."

He locked the door behind the CIA agent and turned, breathing hard. His too-long hair fell into his face, covering his blackened eye. The other gazed at Iris from beneath the shadow of his furrowed brow.

"You don't have to do what he wants," he told her.

She laid her head back, her remaining energy bleeding out of her body. Malignant memories of what she'd just felt from Quinn ate at her soul.

Maddox crossed to her side, settling on the coffee table in front of her. He closed his hand around her knee, his thumb moving gently against the soft flesh on the inside of her leg. A sensation of warmth seeped into her body from his touch.

When he started to remove his hand, she grabbed it, holding his fingers in place. "Don't."

Maddox lifted his other hand and placed it on her other knee. He slowly circled his palms over her knees, the touch light and soothing. "I don't want to hurt you."

"You're not," she said. And it was true. Somehow, whatever pain he was feeling was little more than a buzz of awareness, twinges in her limbs and belly. But the warmth of his hands on her flesh drove those sensations out of her mind.

"I don't know if I'm the man you need watching over you right now, Iris. This thing—" He shook his head, obviously searching for words. "This thing goes deeper than I thought, or Quinn wouldn't have come here."

She caught both of his hands, stilled their movements. "Who is Tahir Mahmoud?"

His eyes narrowed. "I don't know."

She looked down at their entangled hands. "You asked Quinn when terrorists had started using psychics. He admitted he didn't know if they had. That means he already had a terror suspect before he got here, right? A suspect who's somehow led him to the Cassandra Society."

"You're racial profiling, sugar. Don't you know that's a no-no?" Maddox smiled, but she felt no humor from him.

"You looked at Tahir this morning as if you knew him."

Maddox released her hands, but not before she tasted the bitterness of an old, dark rage. "I didn't recognize him."

"But you think you know him."

He pushed to his feet, groaning a little. "You look tired. Rest here and I'll clean up the mess in the bedroom for you."

"Maddox, don't do this."

He gave her a look of feigned confusion. "Do what?"

"Keep secrets from me."

He licked his lips. "Everybody gets to have secrets, Iris. You have secrets, don't you? You kept a real big one from me until just this afternoon."

She looked away, knowing he was right. If his injuries hadn't forced the issue, she probably would still be keeping her ability a secret from him. But that wasn't the only secret she was keeping. She still hadn't told him about the list of names Sharon Phelps had given her that morning at the seminar. It might be her best clue to Sandrine's where-abouts, and she didn't want Maddox or Quinn or anyone else to start making decisions about what she should do with the information.

Maddox took a long, deep breath. "Iris, I don't know for sure who Tahir Mahmoud is. And until I do, I don't want to slander him. Okay?"

She met his gaze and nodded. "Okay." She patted the sofa. "Sit here with me a minute."

Her request seemed to surprise him, but he did as she asked. He felt good against her. Solid. Blessedly painless, to her surprise. Even the rage she'd felt from him was gone.

Relief from the constant agony she'd experienced over the last couple of days washed away what was left of her defenses. Tears followed in its wake, spilling down her cheeks in salty tracks, unstoppable.

"Oh, baby." Maddox brushed at her tears with his thumb, tucking her under his arm. "It's gonna be okay."

She shook her head. "I want to go home," she confessed, the need overwhelming her. "I just want to go home."

He cupped her face. "We can make that happen. First thing tomorrow, we'll get you to the airport and put you on the first flight back to the States. You don't have to stay here."

She put her hands over his. "Yes, I do."

He gave her a gentle shake. "No. You don't. You don't owe Quinn a damn thing. You didn't ask for any of this. It's not your job. It's his."

"I can't leave Sandrine," she said.

"You don't know she's in trouble. Maybe she really is taking part in that focus group, and that's all."

"It's not true," Iris said, blinking back fresh tears. "I know it's not that simple."

She felt it, bone deep.

"Then you go home and let the police handle it." Maddox's voice was firm. "It's their job."

"They don't even think she's missing."

"I'll keep on top of them for you."

She smiled, touched by the offer. "Sandrine's a stranger to you. You might push the matter a day or two, but you don't have any incentive to keep the pressure on. It's up to me." Iris drew away from him. "I'm all she has."

Maddox dropped his hands to his lap. "What about you? Is there someone who can come down here and keep you company?"

"My sister Lily is pregnant. I guess her husband would come down if I asked him to—he's a cop. But I can't ask that of him." She brushed the tears from her cheeks with her fingertips. "My other sister, Rose, is in Colorado with her husband. Daniel Hartman. You may have heard of him."

Maddox arched an eyebrow. "The profiler?"

"That's the one. They're working a serial murder case out there. I can't drag them away just because my old college roommate may or may not be missing." She pushed her hair back from her damp face. "Okay. Enough with the crybaby act. I'll go get the room straightened up and get to bed."

"So, Lily, Rose and Iris," he said, his lips curving. "Bet that was fun growing up."

She smiled. "Flower power, baby."

He tucked a strand of hair behind her ear. "Are the other flowers as pretty as you, sugar?"

She couldn't find her breath, much less her voice. An ache of longing ran through her, as deep as she'd ever known.

When he bent his head toward her, she met him halfway, her lips parting under the gentle pressure of his mouth. He kept the kiss light, his lips moving softly over hers. She curled her fingers in the fabric of his shirt, tightening her grip as the urge to pull him closer and deepen the kiss threatened to overwhelm her good sense.

Maddox dropped his hand. "I'll go clean up the room."

"I can do it." Her voice shook.

He didn't argue, edging away from her.

She stopped halfway across the room and turned back to look at him. He sat half-turned toward her, watching her over the back of the sofa. "Thank you for what you've done for me," she said. "It's way more than most people would."

"Sugar, I was just showin' a little island hospitality. That's all." He shrugged it off, but she felt the ripple of pleasure her gratitude gave him. Strange, she thought, that he'd find such satisfaction in a simple show of regard.

She didn't think he liked himself much, deep down.

MADDOX WOKE to rain drumming the panes of the French doors leading to the veranda. He'd always considered himself a sun worshipper, but over the past two years, he'd grown to love the rat-a-tat of raindrops hitting the banana leaves and dripping from the bougainvillea blooms outside his windows. He liked the way the world smelled after a hard rain, fresh and new.

The clock over the piano read 5:54 a.m. The rain would hold off the dawn a little longer, but he didn't have the luxury of sleeping in this morning.

Not with Iris Browning sleeping in his bed.

It was crazy, but he could still feel her lips on his. Soft as flower petals and twice as sweet. It had taken every bit of strength inside him not to take her into the bedroom and finish what they'd started earlier that day in her hotel room.

How had he let himself get into this mess? It was bad enough to want her so damn badly, but to play bodyguard to her? He'd decided three years ago that his life playing hero was over. He hadn't been very good at it, had he?

People had died because of his decisions.

He rubbed his gritty eyes, listening past the sound of the rain for any sign that Iris might be stirring. Despite her protests the afternoon before, he might be able to persuade her to catch a plane for the States this morning. Mariposa was no place for a woman alone, especially one so obviously fragile.

She was apparently in constant physical pain, beyond what she'd admitted to. He knew what pain looked like, how it etched itself in a person's face. Iris Browning was hurting. Bad.

How much of her pain was coming from him?

He closed his eyes, wondering how such a thing as empathic sensitivity could even be possible. Surely such a thing would have been documented somewhere already if it actually existed—unless people who really do such things took care to hide their abilities from others, he thought. Iris certainly hadn't wanted to tell him that she could feel his aches and pains. He wasn't sure if she'd have said a word if he hadn't called her on it.

She was so different from most of the people he'd run into at the cocktail party and the conference. They liked to talk about their so-called abilities, wore them as a badge of honor.

Wannabes, he thought. Maybe that's why they were still at the conference instead of holed up somewhere playing guinea pig for a former Soviet scientist and his terrorist cohorts.

He shuddered at the thought of Iris putting herself in the hands of Tahir Mahmoud, even with Quinn backing her up.

His cell phone rang. He tried to push himself into a sitting position on the sofa, but the screaming agony in his ribs barely let him stretch his arm out to the coffee table to grab the phone. "Yeah?" he growled.

"It's Darcy." The RSO's clipped tones hinted at a sleepless night. "I thought I'd check on Ms. Browning."

"Mighty thoughtful of you."

"Did you have an uneventful night?"

Maddox couldn't suppress a bark of wry laughter. "Hardly."

"What happened?"

"Now you're interested?" Maddox countered, annoyed at the DSS agent's accusatory tone. "Yesterday you couldn't wait to pass her off to the first beach bum that came along."

"Damn it, Heller—"

"She's fine. Hell, she may have even gotten a little sleep, no thanks to your buddy Quinn."

"What did he do?" Darcy sounded apprehensive.

"Can't tell you that," Maddox said with no small bit of satisfaction. "Classified, you know."

"Is Ms. Browning available to speak to me?"

"She's asleep."

"No, I'm not." Iris's voice made him turn. She stood in the open doorway of his bedroom, dressed in a black silk robe that made her fair skin look like porcelain. His heart dipped.

"Who is it?" She nodded toward the phone.

"Prince Charles."

She shot him a look and took the phone. "This is Iris. Oh, hello, Mr. Darcy."

Maddox tried to make room for her on the sofa, but the slightest movement made him grit his teeth. Iris settled on the edge of the coffee table, giving him a look of concern.

She'd showered sometime since she'd retired to the bedroom; the tang of soap lingered on her skin, the masculine scent rendered exotic and female.

"I really can't say," she said. "You understand."

Maddox grinned, realizing she'd just given Darcy the same runaround on the Alexander Quinn question that he had. Her lips quirked in response, the half smile transforming her face.

His breath caught, trapped in his chest by a crashing wave of desire that caught him flat-footed. He forced himself off the sofa, biting back a howl of pain, and hobbled to the piano bench, putting needed distance between them.

"I appreciate the offer. I'll let you know. Goodbye, now." She disconnected and laid the phone on the coffee table.

"What offer?"

"He suggested I might be more comfortable staying at another hotel and offered to book the room for me under the name of the consulate to preserve my anonymity."

His stomach fluttered. "Maybe you should take him up on it, sugar. Better yet, maybe you should see if he'll help you book a flight back home this morning."

She frowned. "I told you last night—"

"I know what you told me. I also know that Quinn's not going to back off as long as you're here."

Iris jutted her chin, her gaze leveling with his. "Maybe I don't want him to back off," she said.

Chapter Eleven

Maddox stared at Iris, not believing what he was hearing. "You're not thinking of going undercover for him."

"What if I can help uncover a terrorist plot?"

He shook his head. "Who do you think you are, Mata Hari?"

Her lips tightened. "Quinn thinks I can help."

"Quinn's willing to use you. He's not lookin' at you as a partner in crime fighting, darlin'."

She slumped forward, her elbows resting on her knees. "I just want to find Sandrine. Then we can go home."

"I don't think that's on Quinn's agenda."

"That's his problem."

"It's your problem, too, if you work for him." He leaned forward, the movement making his ribs scream with agony. "Ever seen the handiwork of a terrorist attack up close and personal? It's not pretty. You don't want to be on the receiving end."

"Have you?" she countered.

He looked away from her, raking his fingers through his sleep-knotted hair. "Yes."

She was silent long enough to draw his gaze. A look of understanding glimmered in her eyes. "The embassy siege in Kaziristan?" she guessed. "That's how you know Mr. Darcy. And Quinn. You were all there, weren't you?"

"Yeah. We were."

"You were a diplomat?"

The disbelief in her voice made him laugh, despite the fact that humor was the last thing he felt at the moment. "I was part of the Marine Security Guard at the embassy."

Her lips quirked. She reached out and toyed with a piece of his overlong hair. "You with a buzz cut," she murmured.

He caught her hand and kissed her knuckles before letting it go. "You wouldn't have recognized me back then."

"Do you have any photos from that time?"

"No," he lied. He took a deep breath. "Quinn was attached to the embassy, undercover, as a translator. Darcy was an assistant to the embassy RSO, Harlan Brand." Just saying Harlan's name still hurt after all this time. He'd been one of the first to die, in a rocket attack outside the embassy. He'd died trying to protect the ambassador. A hero to the end.

He lifted his hand to brush his hair out of his eyes. His battered ribs howled in protest, making him catch his breath.

Iris released a soft gasp. He looked up and found her brow wrinkled with pain.

"Sorry." His stomach knotting, he rose and crossed to the French doors, putting distance between them.

She followed him to the window, closing her fingers around his wrist. He felt an odd sensation, as if she were drawing him into her, molecule by molecule. "It's okay, I'm used to it."

He pulled his hand away. "I'm not."

She looked away, her face lifted to the pale dawn light seeping through the rain forest outside. "I'm sorry you went through that nightmare. It must have been terrible for you."

The pull of her hadn't ceased just because she'd let go of his hand. He leaned close enough to feel her warmth and pointed to the mountain visible through the glass. "Mount Stanley."

She pressed her nose to the glass like a child. "Strange how you go from a beach to a rain forest on such a small island," she said, apparently content to drop the subject of Kaziristan for now. "I can see why you love it enough to stay."

He chuckled, unnerved by his reaction to her. Not the sexual part; that was predictable. She was a pretty woman in a black silk bathrobe, standing close enough to kiss. But this other feeling, this strange amalgam of admiration and giddy pleasure scared the hell out of him.

He didn't want her to leave. He'd never felt that way about any woman he'd ever brought here.

"How do you afford this place?" she asked.

He wondered how much to tell her. He didn't like to talk about the money. He'd done nothing to earn it, and he had no desire to explain the tainted circumstances of his inheritance. "I came into some money a while back," he compromised.

She turned to look at him. "An inheritance?"

He gazed at the mist-shrouded peak of Mount Stanley. "Yeah."

She didn't say anything else. As the silence between them stretched, he turned his gaze to find her looking up at the mountain, her eyes shimmering with the pale light of dawn.

"You hungry?" he asked.

"Yes." She looked at him. "But don't go to any trouble."

The curve of her cheek gleamed like fine porcelain. He touched her face with his knuckles, almost surprised to find her flesh warm and soft. Her lips trembled apart.

The need to kiss her shook him like a hard wind. Dropping his hand, he backed away, his heart pounding. He entered the kitchen, putting the breakfast bar between them. "I have toast and...toast."

"I'll have toast." Laughter colored her voice.

He dared a look at her and immediately regretted it. She was tempting enough pale and serious; well-slept and smiling, she was dangerous territory. But as she sat on one of the stools on the other side of the breakfast bar, her smile faded. "Maddox, what happened to you?"

He knew what she was asking—what had happened to the spit-and-polish Marine he used to be? How had he ended up in the tropics working odd jobs, cutting all ties to his former life?

He should have known she wouldn't drop the subject of Kaziristan permanently.

"You can't get away from who you really are in the end, Iris. You can try on a different kind of life, but it just doesn't stick." He reached for the pieces of toast that popped up from the toaster, but Iris's words stopped him.

"Who is it that you think you are? Some rough, tough guy who doesn't like to be tied down or care about anyone too much?"

"You tell me. You have it all figured out."

She slid off the stool and walked around the counter to

join him, standing too close for his peace of mind. He didn't want to have this conversation. He didn't want to want someone as much as he had begun to want her.

Nothing good could come of it.

"Kaziristan must have been terrible. Something like that can make you question—"

"Stop it, Iris." He slammed his hand on the counter, relishing the sting in his palm because it distracted him from the queasy knot in the pit of his stomach. "I don't want to talk about it. Talking doesn't change anything. It doesn't undo what happened. It doesn't make any of it go away."

She took a step toward him, trapping him against the counter. She lifted her hand to his chest, placing her palm over his heart. "I can make some of it go away," she whispered.

He felt a tingling sensation in the skin beneath her palm, as if she were drawing his heart out of his chest into her hand. Her brow furrowed, her eyes darkened with pain, but she pressed her hand even harder against his chest.

He stared at her, understanding seeping into his sluggish mind. "It's not just physical pain you can feel," he whispered. He pushed her away from him, stumbling out of the kitchen.

"Let me help you," she said.

"No!" He hunched his back to her, shaking with horror. What had she felt? What had she taken out of him into herself? "You had no right—"

"It's not like mind reading," she said, tears coloring her voice. "I don't know what you're thinking."

"Just what I'm feeling. That's *so* much better."

"Not even that. Not really. I can just feel that you're hurting and I can make it better." Her voice broke. "Please, let me make it better for you."

He made himself look at her. Tears stung his eyes, making him blink. "I don't want you to feel what I feel. It's my pain. *Mine.* I didn't say you could take any of it from me."

She stared at him, her eyes bright with moisture. "You want to hurt? Why? Do you think you deserve it or something?"

He looked away, restless energy flooding his aching body. He crossed to the coffee table and picked up the phone. "You're going home. Today."

"No, I'm not," Iris said, her voice hard as steel.

"Well, you're not staying here. And you're not going back to the St. George." He checked the phone's memory and found the last incoming number. Darcy's cell number. Punching Redial, he waited for the RSO to answer.

"Darcy."

"It's me. Iris would like to take you up on the offer of another hotel room. Can you arrange it?"

"Maddox—" Iris began.

He held up his hand, silencing her. She snapped her lips shut, glaring at him. He turned his back to her.

"I'll book her a room at the Princeton," Darcy said. "I assume you know where that is?"

"Yeah. She'll be there in an hour."

"You do realize the embassy cannot foot the bill for this."

"Yes, I realize that. I'll take care of it."

"May I ask what has happened to lead to this change in plans?" Darcy asked.

"No, you may not." Maddox hung up the phone, slamming the receiver into the cradle.

"I never figured you for a coward," Iris said.

He gritted his teeth, refusing to acknowledge her remark.

"Fine. You run. I'll be in the bedroom, packing." She brushed past him, her warm, lush scent lingering as she slammed the bedroom door behind her.

Maddox dropped to the sofa, closing his eyes. His head was pounding with pent-up anger. Who was she to come into his house and poke her nose into his business?

The bedroom door creaked open a few minutes later, and he heard Iris's soft footsteps approach. "I'm sorry. I went too far. I shouldn't have pushed you."

"Doesn't matter," he said, blessed numbness settling over him like a blanket. "This was a doomed situation from the get-go. I knew it as soon as Darcy suggested it."

"Too much like moss on your rolling stone?" she asked.

He managed a wry smile. "Exactly."

Iris set her suitcase next to the coffee table and sat across from Maddox in one of the armchairs. "You don't need to drive me. I called a cab from the bedroom. They'll be here in a few minutes."

He pushed himself off the sofa, concentrating on the pain in his ribs to keep from thinking about the darker pain in the center of his chest. "Tell them to take you to the Princeton. Darcy'll be waiting."

He crossed to the kitchen counter and pulled the toast from the toaster. It was already cold. He sighed and dropped the bread on the counter.

He felt Iris move closer to him. "I appreciate your

watching out for me last night," she said. "I felt safe here. Thank you for that."

He closed his eyes, wishing he could shut out her words as easily. "You weren't safe at the St. George. That's all."

"I know." Her voice came out low and tight. "You've helped me a lot over the past couple of days. I just want you to know that I'm grateful."

He sighed. "I didn't do anything."

She touched his back, her fingers pressing lightly into the bruises on his rib cage. "Yes, you did." Her hand fell away.

The sound of a horn honking outside made Maddox start. He looked over his shoulder at Iris. "There's your ride." He attempted a smile, hoping it didn't look as sick as he felt.

She retrieved her bag and started toward the door. Maddox caught up with her, realizing he was letting his own conflicted emotions override his good sense. Anybody could be outside waiting for her in that cab, including Quinn.

Or Tahir Mahmoud.

"I'll walk you out," he said, taking the bag from her. He nodded for her to get behind him.

She inclined her head and fell into step behind him, smart enough not to argue.

He relaxed a little when he caught sight of Abner Toulouse behind the wheel of the cab. He and Abner had shot a few tables in the past. He was a good man. "Screw Loose!" He shook Abner's hand as the cabbie got out to help Iris with her bags.

"Mad Dog. Who knocked you around, man?" Abner put the bags in the trunk of the Subaru and cocked his head, a grin spreading across his wizened features.

"Should've seen the other guy," Maddox answered.

"Yeah, yeah, you the big guy." Abner clapped him on the shoulder. Maddox tried not to wince.

Iris opened the back door of the Subaru but stopped before she got into the backseat. She looked at Maddox. "I guess I won't be seeing you again, so, goodbye. Thanks again for everything."

A dull pain started to spread through his chest, stealing his breath, but he pushed it down deep inside him. He didn't want her to feel it and get the wrong idea. "Be careful, Iris. Think about gettin' on the next plane home, like I said."

"I will," she said. He could tell it was a lie. She had no intention of leaving until she found her friend.

He made himself back away from her before he tried to stop her from leaving. She wasn't his problem anymore.

She never should have been.

Abner gave a short wave and drove away, splattering mud behind him. Maddox watched until the Subaru disappeared around the curve and was gone from sight.

"Better this way," he murmured aloud, as if voicing the idea would make it so.

He walked slowly back to his front stoop and sank onto the bottom step, groaning at the agony in his twisted knee. He focused on the pain racing up his leg and into his lower belly, welcoming the burning sensation.

Anything beat the empty feeling in the pit of his stomach.

"ARE YOU CERTAIN you would rather remain here on the island than return home?" Nicholas Darcy asked from the doorway of Iris's new hotel room.

She turned to look at him. He looked so uncomfortable, standing stiff and formal in the doorway. He hadn't even followed her inside, just set her bag on the floor by the door. "I have to keep trying to find out where Sandrine is."

"I thought you knew where she was. Isn't she part of that focus group from the convention?"

"I think there's more to it."

Darcy's eyes narrowed. "Why?"

She couldn't tell him about Quinn, even if Darcy knew who the man was. She had no idea about security clearances or what constituted classified information, so she kept her mouth shut.

"I see," Darcy said after a moment of silence. "Very well. You have my phone number if you need anything. Please don't hesitate to contact me if you have any further trouble. I will do whatever I can to help you out."

"Thank you, Mr. Darcy. For everything."

He gave a small wave and left, closing the door behind him.

Iris sat on the end of the bed and released a long, slow breath. Now what?

She pulled the list of names from her purse and looked at them again. Eight names. An even number—was that significant?

Something Sharon Phelps had said the night of the cocktail party ran through her mind. She'd mentioned that Dr. Grinkov was interested in—how had she put it? Synchronized paranormality?

Synchronized suggested more than one person would be involved. But involved in what?

Feeling restless, she crossed to the window. Unlike her room at the St. George, this hotel room looked out on the street below. She squinted against the bright morning light and peered at the storefronts below. The area looked familiar. Had she been there before?

Then she spotted the faded blue-and-dun sign on the front of one of the buildings—the Sand Dollar Café, the Internet café Maddox had taken her to the other day. Perfect.

Within ten minutes, she was seated at one of the café's computer terminals, a cup of steaming coffee at her elbow. She laid her list of names in front of her and started searching. The first thing she ascertained, pretty quickly, was that of the eight names on the list, only one had a Web site: Celia Shore. None of the others had a Web presence.

However, within a half hour, she'd managed to find mentions of all eight people on the list Sharon had given her, and a pattern began to emerge.

She'd apparently been right about what Sharon had meant by synchronized paranormality. The eight names could be split into four groups of two, based on the purported paranormal specialty of the people on the list. There were two clairvoyants, two telekinetics, two mediums and two empaths.

Well, one empath, since Celia Shore had been a fake.

But what was the significance of the two groups of four? Where did the synchronicity come in?

She tucked the list into the small notebook she kept in her purse and sat back, frowning at the computer screen. There had to be a reason Dr. Grinkov had selected this particular set of people for whatever he had up his sleeve.

Quinn thought terrorists were involved, but Iris couldn't see why, much less how. And until the CIA agent approached her again, there wasn't a lot she could do, was there?

She'd called the St. George to see if Celia Shore's death had affected the conference schedule. The events coordinator told her that the morning sessions had been cancelled, but the conference would resume after 1 p.m.

She had a few hours to kill between now and then.

She started to shut down the computer but stopped, pulling up the search engine page again. She typed in "Maddox Heller" and hit enter. Several links popped up. The first one caught her eye: Concerned Citizens for Maddox Heller.

Curious, she clicked on the link and began reading.

POSEIDON'S COURTYARD lacked the ambience and central location necessary to make it popular with tourists, but locals like Maddox had long since learned about the restaurant's ample portions and friendly service. And everybody loved Moira Reyes, the pretty blond proprietress, whose Tennessee drawl was as authentic as the Southern-style barbecue she and her husband Juan served in their restaurant.

Moira opened the door to Maddox's knock, took one look at his battered face and let out a low whistle. "Good God, what happened to you?"

"Ran into a door," he answered with a smirk.

"Right." To his relief, she dropped the subject, stepping aside to let him in. "Sweetie, it's barely ten. Juan just got the pit fired up. Hope you're not hungry yet."

"Just thought I'd pop in and say hi while I was in the

neighborhood." He didn't tell her what he was doing in the neighborhood; he didn't even want to admit it to himself. In fact, if the shell-pink facade of the Princeton Hotel wasn't staring at him over the treetops beyond the patio, he might even believe it was just a coincidence. But the truth was, he was worried about Iris and kicking himself for running her off from his house when she was obviously in danger.

He sat at a table near the barbecue pit and watched Juan basting the meat already on the grill. "What's up, Juanito?"

Juan flashed him a grin. "My blood pressure, *'mano. La mujerona*, she nags and nags." He softened his complaint with a look of sheer adoration at his wife.

"Yeah, I hear women do that," Maddox drawled.

"If y'all weren't so damned flawed, maybe we wouldn't have to ride your butts so hard." Moira set a glass of iced tea in front of Maddox and sat across from him. "What you need is a good woman, Maddox."

"You just think everybody needs to find his own Juan or Juanita." He grimaced. "Doesn't always happen."

"Well, far be it from me to butt in where I don't belong—"

Maddox couldn't help but laugh.

"Okay, fine," Moira conceded with a grin. "It's my usual M.O. But you're not happy, Maddox. Are you?"

He knew better than to answer the question.

A soft thudding sound drew Moira's gaze to the door. "Don't people read the hours we have posted in the window anymore?" She headed to the front to see who was knocking.

"Moira's right, *'mano*," Juan said, not turning away

from the barbecue pit. "You wouldn't be sittin' here lookin' like somebody ran over your dog if you really liked bein' alone. I don't know why you fight so hard to stay that way."

Maddox had no answer, so he remained silent, letting his gaze wander across the courtyard to the adobe wall, half swallowed by a flowering vine. Beyond the wall, past a line of small palm trees, the Princeton lazed in the hot Caribbean sun.

He wondered what Iris was doing right now.

A faint memory of her scent drifted to him on the warm breeze. He closed his eyes and pictured her the way she'd looked this morning, standing at the French doors before everything had gone to hell.

He could feel the pull of her, that band around his heart drawing him to her.

"Maddox, you have a visitor."

His eyes snapped open at the sound of Moira's voice. Moira stood in the doorway, Iris Browning by her side.

"Maddox," Iris said, her eyes dark with apprehension.

"Hey, brown eyes." He pasted on a knowing grin, hoping it hid the twisting in his gut. "Just couldn't get enough of me?"

Chapter Twelve

Iris looked away from Maddox, heat rising in her cheeks. She should have known better than to come here.

"Seriously, what're you doing here?"

"Are you going to introduce us to your friend?" Moira arched an eyebrow at Maddox, then turned to Iris. "I'm Moira Reyes. This is my husband, Juan. Nice to meet you."

Despite her misgivings about coming here at all, she had to smile at Moira's soft drawl. "You're not from around here."

Moira laughed. "Neither are you. Iris, is it?"

Iris extended her hand. "Iris Browning. And no, I'm just here on vacation." She glanced at Maddox. He stared back at her, unsmiling.

"I bet you'd like some sweet tea," Moira said.

"No, really—you're not open yet—"

Moira waved off her protest. "Be back in a minute."

Iris was tempted to leave anyway, but Maddox's low voice stopped her. "Don't leave on my account."

She squared her jaw and met his gaze. "I have to get to the conference at the St. George."

His smile widened. "That's not for another few hours. I checked."

Now he was really beginning to annoy her. "Planning on gate-crashing again?"

"Maybe."

She sighed. "I thought you were washing your hands of the whole thing."

He didn't answer, his gaze sliding away from hers. Fear radiated off of him like heat, cracking his sarcastic facade. "How'd you find me?"

Iris hesitated. Part of her wanted to turn around and get out of there, go back to the hotel and wait for conference time. The last thing she wanted to do was endure another rejection from Maddox. But another part of her understood his fears, especially now that she'd read about some of what had happened to him in Kaziristan—and afterward.

Taking a deep breath, she crossed to the table where he sat and took the chair opposite him. "I asked Claudell where I might find you. This was the first place he suggested."

Maddox ran his finger around the side of his glass of tea, tracing a path in the condensation. "I wish you'd taken my advice and caught the first plane out of here. I don't think it's safe for you here."

"I told you why I can't leave."

"What good are you doing staying here? You're no closer to finding your friend than you were two days ago, are you?"

"Not really," she admitted. "But I'm hoping Quinn will have some ideas."

"Quinn?" He looked at her as if she'd lost her mind. "You're not doing anything with Quinn."

"Why not?" she countered. "At least he's willing to help me find Sandrine. You've washed your hands of it, haven't you?"

He glared at her, breathing hard.

"Haven't you?" she repeated.

He looked down at the table. "You can't trust Quinn."

"Yeah, well, my track record for choosing who I can trust is a little spotty these days, isn't it?"

He looked up at her, a muscle in his jaw twitching.

"Is there a particular reason you don't trust Quinn?" She had a pretty good idea why he didn't, but she was hoping Maddox would tell her himself.

"We have different ways of seeing the world, that's all."

Nice and noncommittal, she thought. And not enough. She licked her lips and took a plunge. "I know what happened in Kaziristan."

His gaze darkened. "No, you don't."

"No, I guess I don't know everything," she admitted. "But I know more than I did this morning. Did you know there are Web sites devoted to you and what you did during the siege? They call you a hero."

He looked at her, horror in his eyes. "Why did you do that, Iris? I told you to let it go."

"Because you wouldn't tell me, and I needed to know."

He held up his hand, one finger pointing at her as if in accusation. "You don't need to know any of it. I don't want you to know any of it."

"Well, that's too damn bad," she countered, her voice rising more sharply than she intended. She saw Moira turn her head toward their table in response. She took a deep breath and dropped her voice. "I needed to understand where you were coming from. I want to understand you, Maddox."

He looked away from her. "Sugar, you'll be out of here one way or another by the end of the week. What difference could it possibly make to you?"

She knew he was right. She wasn't going to see him again once she returned to Alabama and her life in Willow Grove. She couldn't say why she thought it so important to know what he'd been through in Kaziristan three years ago.

He shrugged before she could formulate an answer. "Hell, maybe it's a good thing. You need to know what kind of sick bastard you're up against if Tahir Mahmoud really is part of al-Adar. Just remember, you can't believe everything you read." His voice dropped an octave. "I'm no hero."

"Yes, you are," she said firmly. "I read firsthand accounts from people you saved during the siege. They all say you got a raw deal from the Marine Corps after what you did to keep those people alive. You shouldn't have been forced out."

"Forced out?" Maddox's laugh lacked any sign of humor. "I wasn't forced out. I resigned. I got the hell out and never looked back. You call that heroic?" He shook his head. "I'm not that guy you read about on your little Web site."

"I know about Teresa Miles. I know what you had to do."

His expression blackened. "What I chose to do."

She tried to cover his hand with her own, but he jerked his hand away. She grabbed the edge of the table, leaning toward him. "You probably don't want to hear this. I'm pretty sure you'll disagree with me. But I think you did the right thing, as horrible and hellish as it must have been for you."

."I could have stopped her murder."

"And gotten a dozen other people killed." Iris shook her head, aching for him. "You know you couldn't have done that."

He slammed his hand down on the table. "Well, I should have been able to do something." Tears glittered in his eyes. "She looked at me. Right in the eye. She saw me watchin'."

Pain, distilled to sharp clarity, ripped through Iris's heart, so distinct, so strong she wasn't sure if it was Maddox's pain or her own. "Maddox, don't—"

"Do you want to understand or don't you?" His voice rose, tight with rage. "This is what happened, Iris. You want so bad to look at it, you're just gonna have to gut it out, because I'm gonna tell you exactly what went down that day."

She sat back in the chair, wrapping her arms around herself. He was out of control now, trapped in a nightmare from his past. He needed to walk through it, step by step, if he was ever going to really escape, and she was just going to have to be strong enough to watch him do it.

She saw Moira start to get up and move toward them, but she met the woman's worried gaze and shook her head. Moira sat down again, gazing toward them with silent concern.

"The al-Adar terrorists hit in a series of coordinated attacks. God knows how long they'd been planning it. They took out Headley—the ambassador—and his security crew first. Brand and Headley survived the car bomb, but the terrorists shot them down while Brand was trying to get the ambassador to safety."

Iris nodded. Those details were in the Web sites she'd read. "You weren't on duty."

His lips curved in a horrible facsimile of a smile. "I'd pulled a night shift and was too keyed up to sleep yet. I was playing poker with a couple of MSGs and one of the embassy's assistant RSOs who was off duty, too."

"Nicholas Darcy."

He nodded. "A third RSO, who was on duty, was killed first thing when the truck bomb hit the embassy. Nine MSGs were taken out at the same time. Only those of us who'd been off duty survived. We split up and started trying to find survivors."

"It must have been chaotic."

He gave a bleak laugh. "Ever waded through body parts? You try so hard not to step on anything—anyone—"

"Maddox—" She clutched his hand, but he jerked it away.

"Cavanaugh took over as acting ambassador when we got word about Headley and Brand. And Cavanaugh ordered everyone to stand down. Stay put. Wait for outside reinforcements."

"But you didn't."

"No. I didn't. See, I'd just found twelve people huddling in a back room. They were scared to go out, but the place was on fire. There was smoke everywhere, terrorists crawling through the place looking for survivors to murder—" A visible shudder rippled through him.

"You were right to ignore the order, Maddox. You saved those people. Your only crime was in making Cavanaugh look bad. He made you the scapegoat to cover his own backside—"

"Stop it, Iris! Stop parroting those Web sites!" He narrowed his eyes. "Don't pretend there's not more to it. If you read those pages, you know there is."

She closed her eyes against the bitterness in his gaze, but he caught her chin and gave her a shake. "Look at me, Iris."

She squeezed her eyes more tightly shut.

He slid his hand around the back of her neck and pulled her across the table toward him. "Look at me."

She made herself open her eyes. He stared back at her, only a few inches away. His agony slid into her, thick and oily, making her stomach rebel. She swallowed hard to tamp down the nausea and held his gaze, knowing she'd asked for the truth.

This was the truth. It wasn't pretty and it wasn't easy, but if he could get through it, so could she.

"Teresa Miles was an interpreter. She was twenty-five. So damned young. She had short blond hair and big green eyes the color of the sea on a sunny day. She was from Iowa. A sweet little corn-fed American girl who just wanted an adventure."

He looked away from Iris, letting go of her neck. She slid back in her chair, watching him through narrowed eyes.

"She got separated from everybody else in her section. I don't know if they ever figured out how."

"She'd gone to the restroom," Iris answered quietly.

He looked up at her. "I never heard one way or the other. They were still investigating everything at the time I got out."

"I guess you haven't kept up with the findings of the congressional investigation."

"No. I testified just before I left the States. I didn't want to think about it anymore." He took a deep breath. "But I can't seem to do anything but think about it these days."

"Is this why you're so suspicious of Tahir Mahmoud? You obviously think he may have been involved in al-Adar."

He rubbed his jaw, his palm scraping against the day's growth of beard. "I think he killed Teresa."

Iris stared at him. "I thought you didn't see her killer. They were wearing head coverings over their faces—"

"The scar on his wrist." Maddox's voice sounded hoarse.

Understanding dawned. "You were staring at it yesterday."

"Teresa's killer had that same scar."

She frowned. "You saw it from where you were hidden?"

"We were hidden closer than you think." He licked his lips, looking down at his glass of tea. "Less than ten yards away. And you know how dark his skin is. Believe me, that white scar was plenty visible."

"Ten yards away," she repeated, horror rippling down her spine. That close—

"Front row seat," he grated. "Arterial blood can really shoot across a room—"

"Stop!"

"It's okay. I'm done." Maddox pushed himself out his chair, stumbling a little as he lurched toward the exit. Iris watched him leave, her heart aching.

Moira got up, reaching out for him, but he shook her hand off his arm and continued out the door.

MADDOX DIDN'T KNOW how he'd ended up sitting in the third-floor hallway of the Princeton Hotel, waiting for Iris Browning to show up. Hadn't he left her at the Poseidon because he didn't want to talk to her anymore? Hell, hadn't he thrown her out of his house to keep her from knowing all his secrets?

Well, it was too late. She knew.

He should've known she wouldn't give up.

But she didn't understand. She bought into that garbage on the Internet, the poor deluded souls who thought that just because a guy managed to get a dozen people out of an embassy siege alive, he was some kind of hero.

But heroes didn't watch a sweet kid from Iowa have her throat cut without raising a finger to save her.

There'd been a way to save her. There had to have been. He'd just been too stupid or scared or gutless to figure it out, that's all.

If only he'd been on duty that morning, and one of the guys who'd died at the gate had been the one at the poker game when it all went down, maybe Teresa would still be alive. Maybe Parker or Hunt or one of the others would have seen how to save her where he hadn't.

Maybe, maybe, maybe. Some days, it seemed that *maybe* was the only word in his vocabulary.

"How'd I know I'd find you here?" Alexander Quinn's gravelly voice jerked Maddox's focus into the present. The CIA agent stood halfway down the hallway, leaning against the wall. Maddox hadn't even heard him coming.

He stood. "You must be psychic."

"I take it she's not here." Quinn said.

"Nope."

"So what happened between last night and this morning, Heller?" Quinn pushed away from the wall and walked slowly toward him, curiosity etched in the fine lines around his eyes. "To bring the lovely Ms. Browning here to a hotel, I mean."

"None of your business."

"Trouble in paradise?"

"Shut up, Quinn."

"The course of true love—"

"I said, shut up."

Quinn smiled. It made him look even more sinister. "She was out of your league anyway."

"She's not going to work with you."

"That's not a decision you can make," Quinn disagreed.

"No, but Iris has been doing a little Web surfing, man. She's learned just how trustworthy you double-O types are." For the first time since she'd mentioned it, Maddox was almost glad Iris had done the Web search into what had happened in Kaziristan. At least she'd taken a cold, sober look at the lengths a government would go to in order to cover its backside when something went all to hell.

"Then she knows about you."

Maddox looked down at the herringbone carpet that lined the hotel corridor, counting the rows out of habit. Anything to keep from thinking too hard about what Iris Browning now knew about him. "Yeah."

"That's good. Maybe she'll be able to knock some sense into you."

Maddox looked up, frowning. "Some sense?"

Quinn shook his head, the look of pity in his eyes making Maddox's stomach twist. "You really have no idea what most people back in the States think of you, do you?"

"I don't care what they think of me."

Quinn laughed. It was worse than his smile. "Why didn't you stand and fight, Heller? You let Foggy Bottom roll over you and you didn't even raise a stink. Why? Did you really buy that garbage those diplomats were peddling to cover their own backsides? Cavanaugh blew it. You didn't."

"I didn't need the State Department PR machine to tell me I screwed up."

"You're not God, Heller. You couldn't save everybody."

"I didn't even try."

"And that was a damn good thing for those twelve people you got out of there alive." Quinn stepped forward, suddenly in Maddox's face. "You know what your real problem is? You're arrogant. You think you're so damn perfect that you should have been able to save everybody."

Maddox grabbed the front of Quinn's shirt. "You don't know what you're talking about," he growled.

"Maybe you should listen to him."

Maddox and Quinn both turned at the sound of Iris's voice. She stood a few feet away, watching their confrontation with her arms crossed over her chest.

Maddox let go of Quinn's shirt. "You don't know what you're talking about either, Iris."

"Probably not," she conceded, her voice desert-dry. "I take it you're both here to see me?"

Quinn smiled at her. Maddox wondered if she found the expression as creepy as he did. "I heard you'd moved out of Maddox's house. I wanted to check on you, see if everything was okay," Quinn said.

"Because he only has your welfare at heart," Maddox added, barely keeping his eyes from rolling.

Iris didn't respond to either of them, walking to her hotel room door and unlocking it. "As much as I'd normally enjoy being the belle of the ball, I'd like to order lunch and have a few minutes to myself before this afternoon's session at the conference. So can we just get to whatever you want?"

Maddox followed her inside, Quinn at his heels. Iris took the only chair in the room, an uncomfortable-looking rattan armchair that matched the small table by the window, leaving Maddox and Quinn to make do with the bed.

Her lips curved as they sat side by side on the floral bedspread, taking pains to keep their distance from each other. Maddox shot her a warning glare, and her smile widened.

"Have you given any more thought to what I asked of you?" Quinn asked.

Iris glanced at Maddox. He shook his head slightly in the negative as he held her gaze.

She looked away from him and back at Alexander Quinn. "I have."

"And?"

"I'll do it."

Chapter Thirteen

"Iris—" Maddox began.

Her sharp look silenced him. She looked back at Quinn. "I don't trust you. I know you see me as a tool in your investigation. But that's okay. I know what to expect. As long as you understand I have one priority, finding my friend. If I can help save other lives as well, I will, but not if it risks Sandrine's life. Understood?"

Quinn's only reaction was a brief nod of agreement.

"It's still dangerous," Maddox said.

She looked at him, wondering why he'd come here after walking out on her at the Poseidon. "I know."

"What makes you think you can get inside the focus group anyway? They seem pretty picky."

"Ms. Browning has an advantage," Quinn said quietly. "She can actually do what she says she can. And whatever they're up to at Telaraña Labs, they seem to need what she can do."

So Quinn had it figured out, too. She shouldn't be surprised. She pulled her notebook from her purse and handed

Maddox the list of names. "This is Dr. Grinkov's focus group. I got it from someone at the conference."

Maddox frowned. "So Celia *was* part of it."

"So was Sandrine."

"Then you know where she is. You can stop worrying."

"You know that's not true."

"You said you weren't a mind reader."

She tamped down her frustration with him and leaned forward. "Quinn's right—something's going on with the focus group. Something big enough and dangerous enough that somebody killed Celia Shore before she remembered anything."

A spark of sheer terror rippled out from Maddox. Iris braced herself as she took the brunt of it.

"I don't think she was supposed to be found alive in the first place," Quinn interjected, earning a glare from Maddox.

"I don't, either," Iris agreed. "Someone took a big risk to finish the job."

"What kind of experiment?" Maddox asked. "I mean, it's hoodoo, not chemistry."

She sighed. "Well, to follow my theory, you'll have to at least pretend to believe in hoodoo. Think you can manage that?"

He clamped his mouth shut and nodded for her to continue.

"I looked into these names." Iris pointed at the list. "These two are clairvoyants—they see things happening elsewhere."

"That's what the C stands for, right?" He pointed to the note she'd made next to the two names. "The T is for what?"

"Telekinetics," Quinn said.

"You've probably heard of Uri Geller," Iris began.

"The guy who could bend spoons?"

"Right. Telekinetics move things with their minds. Knock books off tables, flick light switches—"

"Okay. M is for what—medium?"

"Right. Sandrine is one of two mediums on this list."

"And E must be for empath. Like you and Celia."

"Celia wasn't an empath," she answered tightly.

"She just played one on TV," Quinn added, his voice dry.

Understanding dawned in Maddox's eyes. "She was a fake."

"I think that's why she turned up half-dead. They must have realized she couldn't do what she said she could."

"She knew too much about the experiment to be released unharmed," Quinn said. "But somebody got sloppy. Threw her out before she was dead. They won't make that mistake twice."

Maddox pushed his hair back from his face. "What kind of paranormal experiment is important enough to kill for?"

All Iris had was a theory. She looked at Quinn, wondering if he knew more, and if he'd tell them what he knew if he did.

Maddox slapped his hand on the bed, venting the frustration she felt roiling in his gut. "Somebody talk."

Quinn remained silent, so Iris plunged ahead. "Terrorists are involved. Right?" She addressed the question to Quinn.

He nodded slowly, his expression thoughtful.

She turned back to Maddox. "What do terrorists want?"

"To spread fear in order to achieve their political goals." He spoke as if he were reading from a textbook, but Iris could feel the maelstrom of emotions the mere word evoked in him.

"I've been thinking about the CIA's remote viewing experiments. They spent a lot of money trying to come up with people who could psychically locate a KGB assassin in Europe from the safety of a room somewhere in Langley, Virginia. I bet the KGB was doing something like that, too."

"They were," Quinn conceded. He said nothing further.

"Boris Grinkov was a Soviet scientist before he defected. His area of expertise is actually psychiatry, but he'd have surely known about the KGB's remote viewing experiments. Maybe he even ran them." She looked at Quinn again. He said nothing, but she could tell by his expression that she was right.

More confident now, she continued. "I did some poking around. Dr. Grinkov claims to have some telekinetic ability, though limited, and he's interested in something called synchronized paranormality."

Maddox's brow furrowed. "Synchronized who?"

She couldn't hold back a chuckle. "Pretty much what I said, too. But I get it now, I think." She pointed to the paper. "Four sets of two, each with a different paranormal gift. The word *synchronized* suggests that Grinkov plans to use these gifts in concert to effect some sort of action or event."

"Action? Not just information gathering, then?"

"I think action has to be involved because of the telekinetics. Moving things is what they do."

"Okay, so he wants to move something. Then why does he need the other three?" Maddox asked.

Iris sighed. "This is where it gets weird."

Maddox gave her a look. "It wasn't weird before?"

She couldn't stifle a smile. "I know this sounds crazy. It sounds crazy even to me. But I think I'm right."

"So do I," Quinn murmured.

Maddox slanted a dark look at him. "Right about what?"

"Remote viewing requires clairvoyants. So whatever Grinkov is working on, he wants it to happen somewhere besides Mariposa. Moving objects requires telekinetics. But they can only move things within a certain proximity of themselves. I mean, they can look out the door and move the rake in the yard but not a rake in the yard of some guy in Indiana."

Maddox stared at her as if she'd lost her mind. She looked at Quinn. The CIA agent nodded for her to keep going.

"For the telekinetic to move something in, say, Miami, he'd need the aid of a clairvoyant who could see what's in Miami. But there's no way for them to link their abilities. Not by themselves. That's where I think the mediums come in."

"The mediums? I thought they just talked to dead people."

She smiled again. "They're conduits. Psychic energy flows through them. Yes, they mostly deal with the spirit world, but there are theories, in certain paranormal circles, that mediums really are like pipelines for psychic phenomena."

Maddox's eyes narrowed. "I can't believe I'm sitting here discussing this."

"Join the club," she murmured.

"But you believe in this…stuff."

"I believe in what I know. I know what I can do. I know what my sisters can do."

His eyes widened. "Your sisters?"

"Yes. Lily is a clairvoyant, although she's also sort of, well—" She cut off, not wanting to reveal so much to Quinn.

But of course, he already knew. "Iris's sister Lily can touch people's minds and communicate with them from a distance," he told Maddox. "She found a missing child a couple of years ago. Brought down a senatorial candidate at the same time. That ought to appeal to your antiestablishment streak."

"What about your other sister?" Maddox asked.

"Even more complicated," Iris admitted. "Rose can foresee deaths. Sometimes she can also foresee true love matches—" Once again, Iris cut off the words she was about to say. She could see Maddox's brain overloading. "It's not important."

Maddox rubbed his temples. "Okay, I get how a clairvoyant, a spoon bender and Miss 'I Talk to Dead People' might fit in. But why the empath in this little psychic Goldberg device?"

She chuckled at his description. "I'm not sure. Empaths feel things, and sometimes they can help drain a person of pain or emotion, but I don't see how that helps in the scenario we're discussing." She looked at Quinn. "What do you think?"

"I don't have a theory."

Yes, he did, she thought, but he didn't want to share it with her. The blankness inside him made her stomach quiver.

"Maybe it doesn't connect," Maddox suggested. "Maybe that's why they threw Celia back."

Iris shook her head. She looked at Quinn again. "You sought me out in particular. We both know you know what I can do. I don't think that's a coincidence. Is it?"

Quinn didn't answer.

Maddox turned to Quinn. "Tell her what you know. Now."

"They're an empath short," Iris breathed.

Maddox released a slow breath. Quinn remained silent.

"The only thing I don't get is, how did you seek me out so quickly, Mr. Quinn?" Iris asked.

Maddox smiled, though his eyes glittered with hostility. "Quinn probably knows everything about everyone registered at that conference. If I thought like Quinn—which I don't—I'd pick you, too. You have the job qualifications and the incentive because your friend is missing."

Quinn looked at Iris. "This is important."

"Everything's important," Maddox said. "Oil is important. Shipping lanes are important. Propping up tin-pot dictators is important—"

"Grow up, Maddox. You know as well as I do who Tahir Mahmoud really is. Can we at least concede that?"

Maddox sighed. "I'll concede that. But if you know he's a terrorist, why's he tooling around here free as a bird? Why don't you have him locked up in some Eastern European hellhole, pulling his fingernails out or whatever you freaks do?"

Quinn slanted a dark gaze at Maddox before turning to Iris. "We want to know what Mahmoud and Grinkov are up to. We need inside Telaraña Labs. You can do it."

"Nobody's approached me yet, so why do you think they'd let me in on the experiment now?"

"Mahmoud seemed pretty interested in you," Quinn said.

"Mahmoud wasn't lookin' at her mind," Maddox drawled.

Iris shot him a warning glance.

"We'll just have to set up an exhibition of your talents," Quinn said. "I can go in as a hotel staff employee and set up an accident. Nothing major—just set up a way for you to take away a little pain from somebody in front of the whole group."

Maddox shook his head. "This is insane. You're both insane, do you know that? Iris, you don't know anything about going undercover. And have you forgotten that at least one empath who went into Telaraña Labs came back half-dead, only to be murdered in her own room? You are not going to be Quinn's pawn in this game with Tahir Mahmoud, and that's final."

Iris stood, grabbed his arm and jerked him to his feet. "Excuse us a moment, Mr. Quinn," she grated through clenched teeth, pulling Maddox with her toward the bathroom.

She closed the door behind them and turned to face him. "You're not my keeper. In fact, you made it clear this morning you don't give a damn about me at all, so what the hell do you think you're doing in there, trying to interfere with my life?"

Maddox's eyes narrowed. "I'm trying to interfere with your death, Iris. You have no idea how dangerous Tahir Mahmoud is."

She lowered her voice. "I have a pretty good idea."

"Then you know you don't have any business being anywhere near him." Maddox caught her by the upper arms, pulling her closer. His fingers dug into her flesh, firm but not quite painful. "I'm sorry I kicked you out this morning. That was a mistake. Go pack your stuff and let's go back to my place."

She stared at him, stunned by the unexpected offer. "No."

He let go of her arms, sliding his hands over her shoulder and up her neck to cradle her face. "Why not? You don't want to go back with me?"

The heat of him, the strength of her attraction to him, clouded her brain. Maybe it was the slow stroke of his thumb along her jawline, or the feel of his thighs sliding against her hips as he moved even closer, but suddenly she was having a hard time thinking of a good reason not to go back with him.

"I don't want to waste what's left of our time together worrying about whether or not you're alive." He brushed his lips along the curve of her chin. "Come home with me, baby. Let's start over."

She slid her hands up his chest, curling her fingers in the soft cotton of his T-shirt. "Start what over?"

"This." He kissed her, his lips soft but firm. She clutched at him as the world around her swam into a maelstrom of heat and need. "I want you, Iris," he murmured, his mouth brushing over hers. "Come back with me."

She forced herself to pull away before all her good sense left her. "No."

His fingers twined in her hair. "Come on, sugar, why not?" He tilted her head back, forcing her to look up at him. His voice was low and raspy, sending a surge of desire flooding into her core. "You want this. I want it, too. I've wanted it since the first time I saw you."

She shook her head, fighting the urge to give in to him. "I can't walk away from what Quinn wants me to do."

"Yes, you can." He scattered soft kisses down the curve of her neck. "He can find someone else."

Desire overpowered her, doubly strong as his need

tangled up with hers, swamping her with yearning. Threading her fingers through his hair, she pulled him into another kiss, parting her lips to welcome the slick heat of his tongue against hers.

He lifted her to the sink counter, knocking bottles of hotel lotion and shampoo into the sink with a clatter. He closed his hands over her thighs and drew her legs apart, stepping into the opening until his pelvis pressed flush against hers. He was hard for her, the frantic pulse of his desire racing through her own body, bringing the rapid cadence of her own heart into rhythm with his.

She didn't know where he stopped and she began.

"Come home with me," he murmured against the side of her mouth. "Now."

She fought against the sweet spell of his kisses, aware of what he was doing and why. She put her hands on his chest and pushed him backward. "No."

He struggled briefly against her hands but finally fell back, his back pressed against the opposite wall. He stared at her, breathing hard, his eyes black with need. "Do you want me to say I'm sorry again for this morning?"

"No. I'm not sure I'd believe it anyway."

His eyes narrowed. "What do I have to do to convince you?"

"Telling the truth would be a nice start." She slid off the sink counter, raking her fingers through her tousled hair. "Did you really think you could seduce me out of going undercover for Quinn?"

He didn't try to deny it. "What he's asking you to do is dangerous. I'm lookin' out for you."

That much she believed. "I can't walk away from this. I need to find Sandrine. I need to get her out of there. She'd do it for me, in a heartbeat."

"Then get me into that focus group. Let me go with you."

That one soft plea did more to melt her heart than his apology or his white-hot kisses. "Maddox, you can't. They wouldn't let you in."

"I hope they don't let you in," he said, his voice low and harsh. "I hope they think you're a fake, just like Celia. Maybe I'll start spreading that word around."

The softening she felt toward him hardened into anger. "Don't you dare try something like that."

"You can't keep me from it."

"Quinn can."

His expression shifted as if she'd struck him. She felt a tearing sensation deep in her chest. "You wouldn't do that."

She lifted her chin. "I will if I have to."

She felt a drawing sensation in her chest. Every emotion she'd felt from him drained out of her and into him. He shut his feelings off from her, packed them away somewhere inside him so deep, it was as if he'd never felt anything at all.

"Fine," he said stiffly, turning his back to her. "You do what you gotta do. It's nothin' to me now."

She couldn't seem to draw a deep breath past the pain beneath her ribs, but the ache wasn't coming from Maddox. It was her own pain, raw and deep. She felt as if losing her connection to him had ripped a piece of her out and left her bleeding. She closed her eyes, a toxic cocktail of surprise and regret filling the hole Maddox had left inside her with his withdrawal. "Are you going home?"

He didn't turn to look at her. "What's it to you?" He opened the bathroom door and walked out into the bedroom.

Quinn looked up. "Finished with your heart-to-heart?"

Maddox didn't answer, continuing toward the door. He opened it and walked out, never looking back.

Iris walked stiffly to the chair she'd vacated earlier and sat gingerly, the ache in her chest growing stronger.

"I take it he won't be bothering us anymore," Quinn said.

She met his curious gaze. "Right."

Quinn leaned toward her, his expression sympathetic. But she didn't feel an ounce of compassion coming from him. He was all business on the inside. "It's for the best. He'd get in the way of what you have to do."

"I know."

He stood up. "We have fifteen minutes before the afternoon session starts at the St. George. I'll drive you over and tell you what I have in mind on the way."

MADDOX REVVED the Harley's motor and started up the twisting mountain road at full throttle. The motorcycle bucked beneath him like an enraged animal as it took on the uneven terrain, but he held on and kept going, adrenaline fueling his determination. His anger—at himself, at Quinn, at *her*—whipped through him like the wind on his face, fierce and unrestrained.

The bike hit a skid and he struggled to bring it back under control. After a heart-pounding moment, the Harley pulled out of the skid and back onto the solid track. Maddox slowed down and settled into a smoother, less hair-raising ride.

He'd lost his mind, letting someone he barely knew get to him this way.

Soon he reached the spot he was looking for, a scenic overlook that few besides locals knew about. From that spot on the western face of Mount Stanley he could see most of the western side of the island, from Camelot Beach in the north to Sebastian's hustle and bustle in the south.

The Hotel St. George was a speck of pale pink on the backdrop of sparkling Caribbean blue. It was almost one o'clock. Time for the Cassandra Society's afternoon session.

He gripped the handlebars of his bike, his jaw tightening.

His cell phone rang, vibrating against his hip. He considered ignoring it, but finally gave in, digging it out of the pocket of his jeans. "Yeah?"

"Hello, Maddox." Darcy's clipped tone was unmistakable.

"What do you want?"

"It's not what I want. It's what you'll want."

Unease rippled down Maddox's neck. "What is it?"

"I spoke to one of my contacts in the Sebastian Police Department. They discovered sophisticated sabotage in the St. George's video surveillance equipment."

"Inside job?"

"Quite likely. I'm going to be meeting with the head of hotel security for a late lunch. I thought you might want to be in attendance."

Maddox frowned. "You want me there?"

"I thought it would be of particular interest to you."

It was, but that sort of consideration from Darcy was about the last thing Maddox had expected. It made him uneasy.

Still, he couldn't turn down the opportunity to find out what was going on at the St. George. "What time?"

"Two o'clock at Poseidon's Courtyard."

"I'll be there." Maddox rang off and cranked at the Harley. So Nicholas Darcy suddenly wanted to play nice with him, bring him in on the Celia Shore murder investigation?

Bull. Darcy was up to something. But what?

Chapter Fourteen

The maddening blankness coming from Alexander Quinn did nothing to soothe the fluttering in Iris's belly. He sat behind the wheel of the cab, his sandy hair covered by a brightly colored knit cap that made him look like an island native.

"You're a cold piece of work, aren't you?" she said aloud.

Quinn's green eyes met hers in the rearview mirror. "Yes."

"Guess that's necessary for the job you do."

The corners of his eyes crinkled. "Some of the warmest, most personable people you'd ever want to meet work in the CIA. You've probably met several of them and didn't even know it."

"So you're the exception, then."

He didn't answer, but his gaze shifted a moment, and she felt a twinge of regret before it disappeared into the void she'd come to recognize as Alexander Quinn's soul.

They'd gone over the plan twice already on the way to the St. George. Quinn would create a diversion with one of the rolling carts the hotel staff used to move food in and out of the conference room. Someone would be slightly injured, Iris's cue to take charge and use her gift to ease the hapless victim's pain. It wasn't a perfect plan—what if another empath beat her to it?—but it had the advantage of simplicity.

Quinn pulled the cab into the hotel entrance and stopped by the curb. "I'm going to dump the cab and come back on foot. Get settled in. I'll be there in time for the afternoon break."

Iris stepped from the cab and headed toward the hotel entrance, tamping down a feeling of apprehension purely her own. She managed to smile at the doorman and entered the lobby, shivering as cool air washed over her.

Sharon Phelps was at the reception table again when Iris entered the conference hall. She greeted Iris with a sad smile. "I guess you know about what happened to Celia Shore. We're just all so sad. I think Dr. Grinkov himself is going to be here for the late session to say something about it." Sharon's brown eyes sparkled with excitement. "It's a shame it's taken such a sad occasion to lure him out of his lab. But I'm really looking forward to hearing what he has to say."

"Have you ever met him?" Iris asked, curious.

"Just once, at the national conference a couple of years ago in Dallas." Sharon's cheeks went pink. "He made a point to talk to all the volunteers. He's so kind that way."

Poor Sharon, Iris thought as she found a seat near the center of the conference hall. Worst case of hero worship she'd seen in some time.

She half expected Maddox Heller to slide into the seat beside her, but it remained empty for a long time while the other conference goers settled in for the early afternoon session. Iris slipped her cell phone from her purse and sent a text message to Quinn. "Grinkov here after four. Delay."

A minute later came the response. "Okay."

"I wasn't sure you would be here."

Iris looked up at the sound of Tahir Mahmoud's low accent. "Why wouldn't I be here?" she countered as she slipped her phone back in her purse.

He sat next to her. "I missed you at the afternoon session yesterday. I thought perhaps you had lost interest."

She shook her head. "I had an appointment in the afternoon. I couldn't make the sessions. And, of course, this morning…" She let her words trail off, pushing aside the hum of emotions filtering in from the conference goers around her to concentrate on what Tahir Mahmoud was feeling.

"Sad news indeed," Mahmoud said with the appropriate amount of regret in his voice. Iris even sensed a hint of sadness coming from him, but she wasn't sure she could trust it. If Mahmoud knew what she could do, he might be manufacturing the emotion as surely as Quinn had put on that nasty little terror show for her the evening before at Maddox Heller's house.

The thought of Maddox made her stomach twist into a hard, hot knot. She forced him out of her mind, needing all her energy focused on the plan she and Quinn would put into motion as soon as Dr. Grinkov arrived.

And as disconcerting as she found Tahir Mahmoud's attention, it was probably a good thing that he had decided to make himself her shadow.

He'd be front and center for the show.

POSEIDON'S COURTYARD was packed when Maddox arrived a little before two. On island time, the lunch hour could fall anywhere between noon and three. It had taken Maddox a little while to get used to the laid-back atmosphere of Mariposa after years of precision and discipline in the Marine Corps. He still missed the structure, sometimes, though no one would ever guess.

Nicholas Darcy sat at a table near the back reading a newspaper, one long leg crossed over the other. Despite the heat, he wore an impeccably tailored charcoal suit, a crisp white shirt and a dove-gray silk tie. He was alone.

Maddox waved at Moira as he crossed to Darcy's table and dropped into the chair across from him. "Where's the head of St. George security?"

Darcy put down the paper. "He hasn't yet arrived. Island time, you know."

Maddox narrowed his eyes. "Yeah. Island time."

Darcy met his gaze. "You sound skeptical."

"Why am I really here?"

Darcy tapped the menu in front of him. "Shall we order?"

"No, we shall not." Maddox leaned forward. "Quinn sent you to keep me busy, didn't he?"

Darcy's mouth curved. "I knew you'd see through it."

"So he wants me to do something, but he likes playing games too much to just come out and tell me." Maddox could tell by the look in Darcy's eyes that he was right. "So what's your role in this, then? Keeping me away from the St. George? No, that's too obvious."

"Sometimes a cigar is—"

"—a damning piece of evidence," Maddox finished

for him. "Is the head of St. George security even going to be here?"

"Yes, he is." Darcy looked past him. "Hello, Moira."

"Hi there yourself, English." Moira looked at Maddox, resting her hand on his shoulder. "Your usuals?"

"Yeah," Maddox said. Darcy nodded his assent. Moira left to turn in their orders.

"So is the head of St. George security actually going to tell me anything when he gets here?" Maddox reached for his butter knife, placing it on the table in front of him. He gave the handle a soft thump, making the knife spin.

Darcy's gaze followed the rotating knife. "No. You're not authorized."

"So this really is to keep me out of Quinn's hair." Maddox's butter knife slowed to a stop, the rounded tip pointing straight at Darcy.

Darcy looked up, his gaze direct. "Yes."

Maddox tried to catch Moira's eye to cancel his order, but she was busy.

"I'll tell you what I know," Darcy said, drawing Maddox's attention back to the table.

Maddox eyed him suspiciously. "Why would you do that?"

"Because I know you have a stake in this."

Maddox wasn't sure if the RSO was talking about Kaziristan or Iris Browning. Maybe it didn't matter. "What do you know?"

"It was an inside job. We don't yet know who sabotaged the video surveillance equipment at the hotel, but they were able to get into areas that only authorized personnel can enter. Either the saboteurs were St. George employees, or they had contacts within the St. George security staff. The Sebastian police are following all leads."

"That's hardly news," Maddox said with a grimace.

"Did you know that the same company that provides security for the St. George also provides security for the Princeton?"

Maddox tried to hide his reaction. "Is there a point to this?" he asked, even as he searched his memory for every face he'd seen on his visits to both hotels, trying to make a match.

"I can't intervene in the police investigation. It might even have been unseemly of me to suggest private security to Ms. Browning." One of Darcy's dark eyebrows lifted.

Maddox nodded, the message received. He looked around the restaurant, quickly spotting Moira at a nearby table. This time, he caught her attention. She finished taking the order and returned to his table.

"I'm going to have to cancel my order, Moira. Put it on my tab if it's too late." He stood and gave her a quick peck on the cheek, already moving toward the exit. He reached the Princeton in five minutes, parking the Jeep in the back lot among a scattering of employee vehicles.

One of the benefits of being a go-to kind of guy was that he knew at least one person almost everywhere he went. At the Princeton, that person was Shandra Clendon, a leggy brunette with café au lait skin and eyes the same murky green as Mount Stanley on a rainy day. She worked the check-in counter, her musical Creole accent and ready smile an asset for dealing with demanding tourists.

She rolled her eyes at Maddox's approach. "What do you want now, Mad Dog?"

He leaned against the desk and grinned, making a point of looking her up and down. "Cupcake, that's a loaded question."

Shandra wasn't buying. "I'm busy, Mad Dog. Get to it."

"I met a woman last night and she gave me her room number and told me to come by. I thought I'd surprise her with room service," he said, using the story he'd come up with on the ride over from Poseidon's Courtyard to see just how easily he could gain access to Iris's room. "You know, a little champagne, some chocolate-covered strawberries—"

"Romantic dog," Shandra said with a smile. "What do you want me to do?"

"Can you help me surprise her? She's at a conference at another hotel—the St. George. She should be back by six, and I just wanted to have everything ready and waiting for her. Can you help a fellow out?"

Shandra's milk chocolate forehead creased a moment, then went smooth again, giving Maddox a moment of hope. Then she reached under the counter. "What room number did you say?"

Maddox's heart sank.

AT A QUARTER TO FOUR, the early afternoon session came to a close, and hotel staffers entered the conference hall to set up an informal afternoon tea. Iris saw Alexander Quinn enter the hall at the far end, near the speaker's dais. He didn't look her way, and she didn't let her gaze linger on him.

"In London, afternoon tea is still in vogue," Tahir Mahmoud murmured, leaning toward her as he watched a server approach. "I understand it's not a custom in the States."

"No, it's not," she agreed, trying not to think of who Quinn and Maddox thought Tahir really was. But her skin prickled where his sleeve brushed her arm, and she had to force herself not to recoil.

He motioned to the server, who gave a nod in response. Tahir turned to Iris and smiled. "Since you missed yesterday's afternoon session, I will take it upon myself to inform you that the lemon petit fours are quite tasty, but avoid the scones at all costs."

She made herself chuckle in response, though every instinct screamed at her to run away. "I'll keep that in mind."

A loud clatter nearby plucked her taut nerves, making her jump. A sudden scalding pain raced up her left hand and arm, forcing a whimper of pain between her parted lips. She jerked her head toward the noise. The hotel server stood a few feet away, his hand tucked up against his chest and his face creased with pain. His teapot lay in pieces, hot tea spreading across the linen tray cover and spilling onto the floor.

"He's burned himself!" a woman nearby exclaimed. "Someone send for the hotel doctor!"

As the server made soft, mewling sounds of pain, the phantom pain in Iris's hand deepened and spread, forcing her to bite her lower lip to remain silent.

Tahir Mahmoud hurried to the man's side and led him to a nearby chair. "Someone get me some ice. Quickly!" He looked at Iris. "Do you know anyone who can help him?"

Her heart fluttered, and for a moment, she almost looked

across the room for Quinn to see if she should do something or stay put. But the man's obvious distress wiped away any hesitation. She crossed to the injured man, leaned over him and put her hand on his upper arm, opening herself to his pain.

It raced up her arm and into her chest, setting fire to her nerve endings. She felt herself weaken almost immediately, her legs wobbling.

Mahmoud touched her shoulder to get her attention. She met his gaze, finding him staring at her with a mixture of fascination and cold calculation. He gestured to the chair he'd pulled up for her, and she sat down beside the server.

"How are you feeling?" she asked the man, hating the weak tremble in her voice.

"Better," the server admitted, his brow creasing with confusion. "What are you doing to me?"

"Just helping you stay calm," she answered softly. "Someone will be here with ice soon."

The server closed his eyes, a tremor shaking through him as shock from the burn started to set in. The weakness transferred itself to Iris, making the simple act of keeping her hand on his shoulder almost more than she could manage.

A tall black man in a white coat threaded his way through the crowd toward them, his gaze focused on the injured man. He introduced himself as Dr. Seibling and crouched beside the server. "What do we have here?"

Iris let go of the server's arm and sat back, her whole body shaking with pain and shock. She didn't even have the energy to jump when Tahir touched her shoulder.

"Let me get you away from here," he said softly, his voice

tinged with what sounded like real concern. But when Iris met his gaze, she saw the predatory gleam in his dark eyes.

She shook her head. "I'm fine. I just need a minute."

"I'll get you a drink." Tahir moved away, slipping into the milling crowd. She tried to keep an eye on him, but he was of average height and quickly disappeared from view.

She spotted Alexander Quinn as he came to help clean up the mess from the broken teapot. He glanced her way but gave no sign of recognition. But she didn't doubt for a moment that he'd seen everything that had happened.

The combination of pain and nerves made her head feel fuzzy. She leaned forward in her chair, dipping her head closer to her knees to fight off dizziness. Her whole body started to tingle as if her limbs were falling asleep, the feeling electric, disconcerting and invasive.

"Miss Browning?" An accented voice filtered through the white noise rushing through her head. She forced herself to sit up and open her eyes.

A tall, slender man in a gray tweed jacket stood before her, his ice-blue eyes fixed on her face. One eyelid twitched sporadically, the haphazard cadence mesmerizing. Strong Slavic features under a thatch of hay-colored hair hinted at his ancestry, and Iris knew, instinctively, she was looking at Dr. Boris Grinkov.

THE VIEW from the balcony of Iris Browning's room at the Princeton Hotel was hardly the stuff of picture postcards, Maddox thought. The street below was dusty and crowded with tourists emerging to enjoy the late afternoon sunshine. The faded storefronts were quaint and shabby, the sandstone facades crumbling in places. The store owners would get around to repairs when tourist season began to die down. Maybe.

He walked back into the room, closing the balcony doors behind him to shut out the street sounds. The silence closed around him like a shroud, making it hard to breathe as he sat on the edge of Iris's bed.

Getting into her room had been dishearteningly easy. The right story to a sympathetic ear was all it took. If Tahir Mahmoud hired a local with the right contacts to do his dirty work, Iris could easily be dead before anyone could stop it.

He closed his eyes. Images filled the darkness, painted in vivid colors across his memory. Teresa Miles, struggling against the black-clad arm that held her prisoner. Her blue eyes staring right into Maddox's where he hid with the others under his guard, helpless to stop what happened next.

The flash of steel as the knife whipped up to Teresa's throat—

"What are you doing here?"

He snapped his eyes open, nausea writhing like snakes inside him. Iris stood in the doorway, as pale as death.

He pushed himself up from the edge of her bed, his planned safety lecture forgotten. "Are you okay?"

She looked away from him, but her fingers tightened around the door frame. "I'm fine."

"No you're not," he realized. He reached her side, lifting his hand to her cheek. She felt cold. Dark circles bruised the skin under her eyes, and her lips were bloodless. She swayed into his touch, and he caught her before she fell.

He lifted her into his arms, alarmed at how fragile she

felt, and carried her to the bed. He laid her atop the comforter and sat next to her, pushing her tousled hair away from her forehead. "Oh, baby, what happened?"

She told him about the server's accident and what she'd done. "I got what I wanted. Grinkov's attention."

Maddox put his hand over her lips. "Shh. We can talk about this in a few minutes. You're about to pass out on me here. Have you eaten anything since breakfast?"

A wry expression flitted over her face. "I never had breakfast, remember? You kicked me out before we ate."

Guilt burned a hole in his gut. He dialed the room service number posted by the phone and ordered an omelet and toast.

"I'm not hungry," she protested, struggling to a sitting position.

"Too bad, because you're eating something anyway." He cupped her chin in his palm, sliding his thumb over her bottom lip. "Still in pain?"

Her eyes fluttered closed, her lip trembling beneath his touch. She shook her head.

Desire jolted through him, fierce and unbidden. He dropped his hand quickly and started to get up, but her hand closed around his arm, her grip stronger than he expected.

"Don't go," she said softly.

He met her gaze, his heart pounding. "Iris—"

"Stay with me," she said.

Resistance melting, he settled back on the bed, his hip against hers. He took her hand in his. "What am I going to do with you, baby?"

"What do you want to do with me?" she asked, her gaze unflinching.

His heart rate ramped up to a gallop. "Sugar, you're in no condition for what I want to do with you."

Her lips curved, and she released a soft laugh. "Maybe after the omelet."

He laughed, surprised at the devilish gleam in her dark eyes. "You're full of surprises, sugar."

She twined her fingers through his. "That's a good thing, isn't it?"

He nodded, lifting her hand to his lips and pressing a gentle kiss on her knuckles. "It is."

"Do you want to hear about my meeting with Grinkov?"

A dark thread of anger weaved its way into him, but he tamped it down. "Yes, I do."

"Dr. Grinkov invited me to join the focus group."

Apprehension coiled in Maddox's belly. "When?"

"Tomorrow morning," she said.

Chapter Fifteen

"I don't want you to go," Maddox said quietly.

Iris looked up from the half-eaten omelet. "I have to go."

He shook his head, settling on the side of the bed beside her. "Quinn can find someone else. Look at you." He gestured at the fork trembling in her hand. "You need to rest."

Frowning, she laid the fork on her food tray and tucked her hand in her lap. "I'm fine. The shower helped. I just shouldn't have gone so long without eating."

His voice roughened. "I don't want to find you washed up on the beach in a day or two."

"Celia was a fake," she protested. "I'm not. I can do what they want me to do. They need me."

"You don't know what they want." He touched her knee, the warmth of his touch seeping through the silk robe, making her acutely aware of the fact that, other than her robe and a pair of panties, she was naked. Her sudden awareness of him almost eclipsed the anxiety pouring into her from his gentle touch.

She closed her hand over his. "I know you're afraid for

me. I appreciate it more than you know. I'd feel very alone right now if you weren't here."

He cradled her hand between his palms. "I talked to Nick Darcy today. The tampering with the surveillance tape at the Hotel St. George looks like an inside job. And that same company provides security here at the Princeton." He lowered his voice a notch to a rough growl. "It took me less than a minute to talk my way in here, Iris. If I can do it—"

She squeezed his hand. "Stop trying to scare me."

"You need to know what kind of people you're dealing with."

A ripple of terror washed through her from where his hands cradled hers. He snared her gaze with his, leaving her with no doubt he intended for her to feel everything he was sharing with her through his touch.

"Stop," she choked, tugging her hand away.

He let her go. "I'm sorry. I'm not trying to hurt you."

She cradled her hand to her chest, fear still churning inside. "Are you sure about that?"

He brushed her jaw with his fingertips. The touch was light, soothing and free of pain, though it evoked a twisting sensation in the center of her chest. "I'm sure."

The low rumble of his voice sent tremors up her spine. Need coiled into a tight knot. She reached for her fork, trying to distract herself from the onslaught of desire, unsure what part of the sensations were coming from Maddox and what was hers alone.

He retreated from the bed and stood by the balcony doors, leaving her to finish the omelet and toast in silence. But his emotions filled the room like white noise, buzzing through her brain as she washed down dinner with a glass of orange juice.

When she was finished, she broke the silence. "Why did you really come here?"

"I told you, sugar. You're not safe."

"And that's all?" She started to put the empty tray on the bedside table, but he intercepted it, taking it from her hands.

He put the tray outside the hotel room door for room service to retrieve and turned back to her. "I let you down this morning. I want to make that up to you."

He sounded so serious, she thought, miles from his usual snarky self. "You don't owe me anything."

He sighed. "You want me to leave?"

"No." She stretched a hand out to him. "Sit with me."

He closed the distance, taking her hand. He stared at their clasped hands for a moment, then lifted his gaze to hers, his eyes dark with questions. She moved closer to the edge to make room for him next to her.

His body felt warm and achy as he settled in beside her. She ignored the twinges of pain from his bruises and scrapes, focusing instead on the electric feel of him next to her. The pain started to fade away to nothing.

She leaned into his body and he shifted, sliding one arm around her to tuck her against his side. She laid her cheek against his chest and listened to the thud of his heartbeat, steady and a little fast.

"You look like you could use a good night's sleep," he said in a growly half whisper.

She smiled. "Such flattery."

He smiled back. "I guess I should stick to being the strong, silent type, huh?"

She smoothed a wrinkle in his shirt. "Big, tough Marine."

He didn't answer, drawing her gaze. A frown creased his forehead as he stared at the far wall.

"Why'd you join the Marines?" she asked.

His chest rose and fell in a deep sigh. "Because becoming a nuclear physicist just wasn't in the cards."

"Seriously."

He ran his hand over his chin, his palm rasping against his beard stubble. "I was tired of being everybody's mistake."

She pushed up to look him in the eye. "You're not anybody's mistake."

"My father would've told you different."

"Your father thought you were a mistake?" She hid her reaction to the pain emanating from him in bleak waves, afraid he'd close up if he knew he was hurting her.

His smile was terrible. "Ever heard of Alton Sinclair?"

"The billionaire guy who left his money…" She trailed off, gazing up at him with dawning understanding. "You were—"

"—the bastard son he used to shaft his legitimate heirs."

"So you really do have a trust fund," she murmured, remembering something he'd said the first day they met.

He looked away. "I tried to give it back to them. But when they wouldn't even meet with me, I just said forget it. They don't care enough to meet me, why should I care whether they can afford a new vacation home or this year's Porsche?"

His bitterness burned like fire along her nerve endings,

but she gritted her teeth and held on. "Your father must have wanted you to have it—"

His bleak laugh made her shiver. "He didn't want me to have it. He just didn't want them to have it."

"He could have given it to charity."

"But that wouldn't punish his kids enough." He sighed again, his breath stirring her hair. "Just proves he never even bothered to get to know me. I mean, if he thought his other kids were screwups…hell, I messed up a lot as a kid, too. I was so angry at everything. Always in trouble."

"Did you choose the military or was it chosen for you?"

He looked down at her, smiling. "A little of both."

"So the Marines straightened you out?"

His dry laughter rumbled against her cheek. "I'm a beach bum, baby. Do I look straightened out to you?"

She sat up. "You're not a bum, Maddox. You're a hero."

"Iris, I'm not—"

She pressed her fingers to his lips, shushing him. "I'm not even talking about what happened in Kaziristan. I'm talking about what you did for me." She traced the curve of his lower lip, fire smoldering inside her. "I didn't know what to do or who to go to, but you were there for me, and you didn't have to be. That's not the act of a bum."

He kissed her fingertips before tucking her hand to his chest. "You have a low threshold for heroism, baby." He started to get up from the bed.

"Where are you going?"

"I'm just going to settle in the chair right over there and let you get some rest."

She caught his arm. "I thought you were going to show me what you wanted to do with me."

He settled on the bed, his gaze intense. "Iris—"

She angled her chin at him. "I know you want me."

He cupped her jaw. "I do," he admitted.

She licked her lips. "Then what's wrong?"

"Just because I want something doesn't mean it's right." He smiled wryly. "Usually, it's just the opposite."

She cradled his face between her hands. "Not this time." She bent and touched her mouth to his.

He kissed her back, lightly at first, his lips soft and curious. But when she touched her tongue against his lower lip, he curled his hand around the back of her neck and pulled her close to him, until her breasts flattened against the hard wall of his chest. He dropped his hands to her hips and pulled her into his lap, parting her thighs until she straddled him.

Heart racing, she slid closer, until the hard ridge of his erection pressed into her softness. A low whimper rose and died in her throat as his hips shifted upward in response.

"Are you sure about this?" he murmured against her throat.

"Yes," she whispered.

He slid the hem of her robe upwards, baring her skin to his touch. His thumbs stroked her inner thighs, sending white-hot need racing up her nerve endings.

His hands moved slowly up her legs, until his fingers brushed the silk of her panties. She bit her lip as his face grew still and focused, his gaze following the movement of his hands against her flesh. His intensity was both exciting and unnerving, and she trembled wildly when one thumb found her center and began to stroke her through the fabric.

He lifted his gaze to hers. "Do you like that?"

She couldn't find her voice, but her wobbly nod made him smile. He started to withdraw his hand but she caught it in hers, holding him in place.

With his free hand, he tipped her chin, forcing her to look at him. "This isn't a race, baby. Slow down."

She let go of his hand, her heart galloping in her chest. His eyes narrowed. "You've done this before, right?"

"Yes," she said quickly, then added, "once."

"Prom night?"

She chuckled. "College boyfriend."

"Just once, huh?" He didn't shift his gaze from hers, but he ran his hands soothingly over her shoulders and down her arms, his fingers leaving a trail of fire that branded her through her silk robe. "Either it was so memorable you didn't want to risk being disappointed with the next time, or…." He dropped his hand to the knotted belt of the robe.

"Definitely the latter," she admitted, her gaze following the sinuous movements of his fingers as they untied the sash.

"Bet he was a frat boy," Maddox murmured in a tone of amused contempt. He tugged at the belt and pulled it loose. The edges of her robe fell open, baring her flat stomach and the hollow between her breasts.

"Yes, he was." She took a swift breath through her nose as he lifted one hand to the lapel of her robe and pulled it aside, uncovering her right breast. He grazed his knuckles over her nipple, sending a sharp ache shooting through her.

He looked up at her quick intake of breath. "Can you feel what I'm feeling, too?"

She didn't know if the heavy ache between her thighs was all her own or something she was sensing from him. Little twinges of pain from his scrapes and bruises flickered in and out of her consciousness, but the other sensations flooding her swallowed them up like sharks feeding on minnows.

She felt hot all over. Her skin prickled, perspiration glistening on her bared skin. She touched the center of his chest and felt his heart racing in cadence with her own, his breath rapid and fierce. A feral restlessness settled in the pit of her belly, tight and hot.

"I don't know," she admitted, meeting his gaze. "I don't know what's you and what's me."

A low growl escaped his throat. He lifted his hands to her shoulders and pushed aside her robe. Dipping his head, he covered one nipple with his mouth and suckled lightly. She threaded her fingers through his hair and held on, shaken by the electric pulses racing through her body where his lips touched.

He dropped his hands to her thighs again, his thumbs resuming a slow, circling path up her legs until he reached her panties again. This time, he slipped one hand underneath the fabric and cupped her in his palm, the heel of his hand pressing firmly against the sensitive knot of nerves at her center.

He lifted his mouth from her breast, his forehead resting against her collarbone. He slipped a finger inside her, chuckling softly at her gasp. "You like that, too, huh?"

She was helpless to stop the slow thrust of her hips against his hand. "Yes. Please…"

He kissed her breast. "I want you so much, Iris. You know that, don't you?"

"Yes," she breathed, her head falling back. Pleasure stole over her, as relentless as an ocean tide.

"That's it, baby. Just let it happen." Between her legs, his fingers wrought dark magic. Heat bloomed at her center and spread outward, setting off tremors in her thighs and belly.

She dug her fingers into his upper arms, a guttural groan rumbling through her chest as she unraveled beneath his touch. She felt hot, then cold, her heart slamming hard and fast against her rib cage. And still Maddox stroked her deeper into madness, murmuring soft words of encouragement as she rode an even longer wave of pleasure.

She collapsed against him, her head resting in the curve of his neck. Her breathing was rapid and harsh, edged with a low keening sound she hardly recognized as her own voice.

"Do you want to stop here?" he whispered in her ear, the soft words edged with fierce need.

She found the strength to lift her gaze to his. She shook her head slowly. "No. Don't stop."

He sat back and reached for the zipper of his jeans.

She caught his hands and pushed them aside. Holding his gaze, she unzipped the jeans herself and slipped her hand inside, closing her fingers around him through his briefs. He uttered a heartfelt oath, making her smile.

"You like that?" she asked, feeling deliciously wicked.

"Oh, yeah." He laughed softly, but his expression bordered on agony as she stroked the length of him through the thin cotton. "I like that a lot."

She slipped her hand inside the briefs and took him

fully in her hand, both shocked and thrilled by her daring. "How about this?"

Furrows appeared between his eyebrows and his eyes fluttered shut. He made a low, growling noise that she took as an affirmation.

She realized, with sudden dismay, that she didn't really know what to do next. Her touch faltered, her hand shaking.

Maddox opened his eyes and looked at her. "What's wrong?"

She withdrew her hand, hot tears burning her eyes. She looked away.

Maddox caught her face between his hands, forcing her gaze up to meet his. The tenderness in his eyes brought the tears spilling down her cheeks. "It's okay. We don't have to—"

"It's not that," she said quickly. "I just don't know—"

He shushed her with a light kiss. "You're doing fine."

"I know this was my idea—"

A smile curved his lips, carving dimples into his cheeks. "I don't know about that, sugar."

She laughed despite her growing mortification. "You're a nice guy, you know that?"

He shook his head, his hands settling on her hips. "Actually, I'm a naughty guy. I thought you knew that by now."

"I do want this, Maddox." She pressed her palm to the center of his chest, allowing herself to draw on the sense of calm she saw in his face. He exhaled softly, his expression shifting as if he realized what she was doing.

She started to remove her hand, but he trapped it against his chest. "It's okay."

He let go of her hand, and she reached down and tugged the hem of his T-shirt upwards, baring his flat belly. He was sun-bronzed and well-toned, the conditioning he must have received in the Marine Corps still evident. He helped her pull the shirt over his head, then returned his hands to her hips and sat quietly, awaiting her next move.

She ran her fingers over the tattoo of a snarling bulldog and the letters USMC that blued the skin over his heart, then bent and kissed the tattoo.

He cradled her face and drew her up for a long, deep kiss.

He whispered words of encouragement as she helped him remove his jeans and boxers. He eased her panties down her legs, kissing her from hips to ankles and back up again. He pressed soft kisses against her lower belly, stroking her lightly between her legs with two fingers.

He moved up her body, dropping kisses along her rib cage and over her breasts. He rolled away from her long enough to retrieve a condom from his wallet. She lay back against the pillows and watched him sheath himself, her heart pounding.

What was she doing? Why was she here, naked with this man she'd met only days before, on the eve of the most dangerous thing she'd ever done in her entire life?

Maybe that was why, she realized as he settled his body over hers, his dark blue gaze as fierce as the pounding of her heart. Maddox made her feel safe. He cared whether or not she made it out of the Telaraña lab alive.

He might be the only person on the whole island who did.

Night fell like a whisper, surrounding them with shadows as they made love. Time melted into a riot of sensations, both hers and his, each one building on the other, twisting and twining until Iris couldn't tell where her body ended and Maddox's began. He was both gentle and demanding, pushing her deeper into the sweet heart of madness with each kiss, each touch, each roll of his hips. She rose to meet the challenge of his passion, giving as much as she got, until she plunged over the edge once more, taking him with her this time.

She hadn't thought she could sleep that night, with thoughts of the coming trip to Telaraña Labs heavy on her mind, but nestled in the curve of Maddox's strong arms, she found the first real rest she'd known in days.

MADDOX WOKE to an empty bed. He blinked away sleep and pushed up on his elbows, looking around the dark, unfamiliar room until he spotted Iris's silhouette by the window, softly outlined by the golden lamplight from the street below.

He rolled off the bed and crossed to her side, closing his hand over her shoulder. She jumped, whirling around to look at him. He could barely make out her wide eyes in the low light. "Sorry, didn't mean to scare you."

She remained tense. "I guess your knee is feeling better."

The cryptic remark threw him. "Actually, it's killing me."

She stared at him a moment, her expression unfathomable. Then she turned and looked out the window. When she spoke, her voice was distant. "It's starting to rain."

The cool tone of her voice made his stomach clench. He

took a deep breath and brushed a tousled lock of dark hair away from her neck. "Sure you don't want to stay here instead? Lovely weather for lying in bed all day."

"I can't. I should go shower. I'm supposed to meet the Telaraña Labs shuttle in front of the hotel at eight." She slid away from his grasp and crossed to the bathroom. She flicked on the light, and he caught a glimpse of her pale face and dark, haunted eyes before she shut the door behind her.

He walked slowly back to the bed, his gut twisting with unexpected dismay. Her change of mood had caught him flat-footed. She'd seemed happy and relaxed after they'd made love, curling like a kitten in his arms, her sleepy smile making his heart turn flips.

But maybe with dawn had come regrets. She barely knew him, and by her own admission, she wasn't a woman with any real sexual experience. Maybe she'd let nerves and hormones overcome good sense and was now kicking herself for it.

Maybe he'd been nothing but a distraction after all.

He dropped heavily onto the bed, gazing at the closed bathroom door. The sound of the shower mingled with the soft drumming of rain against the window, a melancholy symphony washing over him like a cold draft. He found his T-shirt and pulled it over his head, trying to ignore the slow ache spreading like poison through his chest.

It was only much later that he thought to wonder why Iris hadn't felt the throbbing ache in his knee.

Chapter Sixteen

Don't panic, don't panic, don't panic!

Iris stared through the windshield of the shuttle van at the soggy gloom of the rain forest surrounding the base of Mount Stanley. On the tiny island of Mariposa, the drive to anywhere was a short trip. Iris needed more time to process the truth she was only now beginning to admit to herself.

Her gift was gone.

She had felt nothing when Maddox approached her that morning at the window of her hotel room. Not a knee twinge, not a sting from his cuts and scrapes, not even a scintilla of whatever emotions he'd been feeling as he touched her shoulder.

It was like being deaf and blind at the same time.

She couldn't remember a time when she wasn't aware of what other people were feeling. Around age seven, she'd come to understand that all those extra sensations swirling in and out of her weren't shared by other people. It had been a scary moment for her, realizing she wasn't like everyone else.

Sitting there in the shuttle van, completely insensate to

all but her own mild aches and pains from her night with
Maddox, she relived that same sense of fear. Only this
time it was because she was just like everyone else.

Don't think about it.

But how could she not? She was about to walk into a
dangerous situation without the one weapon she'd thought
she'd have at her disposal. The one thing that would keep
her from being thrown into the ocean just like Celia Shore.

What had happened? Why had the gift left her now,
when she needed it more than she ever had before? Could
the answer be as simple as making love with Maddox?

But she'd had sex before, and while no, it hadn't rocked
her world, surely that couldn't be enough to strip her of a gift
that had been a part of her life for as long as she remembered.

A bubble of hysterical laughter rose in her throat. She
swallowed it quickly, glancing at the van driver to see if
he'd noticed. He was a burly, taciturn Creole with a per-
petual grimace, the antithesis of the smiling, garrulous
Mariposans she'd met during her brief stay. If he'd heard
her aborted laughter, he gave no sign of it.

Iris settled back, closed her eyes and tried to feel something—anything—from the driver. But he was still a blank.

"We're here." The man's voice made her jump. She
opened her eyes and took in the squat cinder block mon-
strosity ahead, sprawling over a large clearing hacked into
the rain forest. It was only one story tall and painted the
same deep emerald as the trees surrounding it, tan block
letters spelling out TELARAÑA LABS the only break in
the unrelenting expanse of green.

Nothing says incognito quite like an ugly green paint

job, Iris thought as the van driver pulled to a stop in the narrow parking strip outside the front entrance. He motioned for her to get out and went around to the back to retrieve her bags.

She was beginning to regret turning down Maddox's suggestion of a lazy day of lovemaking.

At least the rain had slowed for now, though misty clouds hung low overhead, promising more precipitation. It was ten degrees cooler here in the mountains than it had been back near the beach, and Iris was glad she'd thought to carry a light cardigan. She shrugged it on and followed the Mariposan driver as he carried her bags to the front door.

A small surveillance camera—also painted green—eyed them from the small awning over the front door. The driver set down her bags, pushed a small intercom button by the door and looked straight into the camera. Seconds later, a buzzer sounded, and the driver pushed open the door. He retrieved the bags and gave Iris a curt head gesture to go in first.

The driver set her bags down next to her and walked back outside without a word, leaving her standing alone in the barren lobby, which was little more than a narrow hallway with a table and chair set against one wall. It was unoccupied.

She waited a moment, her heart pounding, before she worked up the courage to speak. "Hello?"

Silence answered her.

She stepped forward, looking down the hallway in both directions. Several doors, all closed, lined the corridor. She stood very still and again tried to feel something besides the tremble of her ragged nerves and the pounding of her heart in her chest.

A soft tapping sound to her left drew her attention. A man rounded the corner and stepped into the dim hallway. Backlit by the single dome light at the end of the hall, he was little more than a silhouette moving toward her at a steady, un-hurried pace. But as he drew closer, she recognized his too-slim frame, slumped shoulders and unruly straw-colored hair.

He stepped into the circle of light cast by another dome lamp positioned in the center of the lobby area. His icy eyes met hers and he extended his hand.

"Welcome to the Telaraña laboratory," Boris Grinkov said.

MADDOX REACHED the Tropico within five minutes of Alexander Quinn's terse call and went inside, unsurprised to find the place doing a brisk business three hours before noon. He ordered a small beer to mollify Theodore, the burly Mariposan bartender, and left it untouched at his elbow while he waited for Quinn to arrive.

The CIA agent entered precisely at the appointed time, dressed in a faded blue T-shirt, a pair of well-worn jeans and a red bandanna wrapped pirate-style over his head. His snakeskin boots thudded heavily on the plank flooring as he made his way to Maddox's table and straddled the chair across from him.

"Another body has shown up," he said without preamble.

Maddox frowned. "Someone else from the focus group?"

"Andrea Marquez. The second empath."

Maddox tried not to react, but his blood felt like ice in his veins. "Murdered?"

"That's not clear yet. I have an inside man on the lab's cleaning crew. He'll be going out this morning with the rest of the crew to makes sure Iris is okay."

"You have to get her out of there."

"She should be okay for now. As long as she can do what they need her to do. Which we both know she can."

Maddox frowned, something niggling at his brain. "I don't like it," he said aloud.

"If we move too soon, we'll lose this chance to find out what Mahmoud and Grinkov are up to."

"And if we move too late—"

"We won't."

"You can't know that. What if she gets in there and freezes up? Or what if she can't do what they expect—" The thought that had been lurking in the back of his brain rushed forward. "Oh, God. She didn't feel it."

Quinn frowned at him. "What?"

"This morning, before she left. My knee was killing me when I woke up, but she didn't feel it." Dread slithered through Maddox's gut.

Quinn's silence was scarier than anything he might have said. He looked down at the scuffed barroom table, avoiding Maddox's gaze.

"You've got to get her out. Today."

Quinn shook his head. "My man's not trained for extraction. He's only supposed to make contact to see if she needs anything."

"Then send in someone else."

"This isn't the States. I can't just call up an extraction team on a whim. It'll take time."

"She may not have time."

"And I don't want another hostage situation," Quinn added quietly, looking pointedly at Maddox. Silence stretched between them a moment, then Quinn added, "There's another possibility."

A wave of cold nausea rippled through Maddox as he realized what the CIA agent had in mind. "No."

"You have the training. You've done it before."

Maddox shook his head. "You must have other people—"

"Not in place. And she trusts you."

Maddox pushed to his feet. "She shouldn't!"

The other bar patrons turned and stared at his outburst.

Quinn grabbed his arm and pushed him back toward his chair. "Sit down and get a grip."

Maddox was glad he'd skipped breakfast.

"WE HAVE a session planned in twenty minutes in the conference room," Grinkov said, setting her bags on the floor of the small, private dormitory room he'd led her to after greeting her at the entrance. "I'm afraid you'll have to unpack when you're finished."

"And we'll be working on an actual experiment this morning?" Iris asked, tamping down her rising panic. So far, her empathic sensitivity was still out of commission, and her complete inability to read Grinkov's guarded body language wasn't doing much for her sense of confidence.

"I have one set up, yes. We shall see how it goes." On the way to her room, Grinkov had briefly sketched for her the focus of his research. As she'd surmised, he was attempting to create a sort of psychic network, with the medium linking the clairvoyant and the telekinetic to see if it was possible for the group to affect objects at a distance.

Grinkov led her down another of the long, quiet corridors that seemed to characterize the lab, at least as far as she had seen. The conference room was at the end of the hallway. Grinkov opened the door, his gesture for her to enter ahead of him the picture of courtliness.

Inside, a rectangular table filled the center of the cramped room. Two women and a man sat at the table. Bottles of water sat in front of each of them, and there was a fourth, unopened bottle in front of the single empty chair at the table.

All three sets of eyes turned toward her as she and Grinkov entered. Self-conscious, she walked slowly to the empty chair and sat, closing her fingers around the water bottle, focusing on the cold, wet feel of the condensation beading on the plastic to distract her from her growing panic.

Grinkov made quick introductions—the man was Tom Stanton, the women Hildi Jennings and Bailey Floyd— then went to a small desk near the corner of the room, where a video monitor and a stack of papers filled most of the battered wood surface.

The other group members looked at Iris silently for an uncomfortable moment. Even without her empathic gift, she couldn't miss the suspicion and curiosity radiating from them.

Hildi broke the silence. "You must be the new empath."

Iris nodded. "And you're—?"

"Clairvoyant." She nodded at Tom. "Medium."

"And I move things," Bailey interjected dryly in a flat Texas drawl.

"I hope you're a better empath than the last one," Tom said, his voice as dry as Bailey's.

"Who was the last one?"

"That crazy TV psychic wannabe. Celia Shore." Bailey poked at her water bottle. "She was useless."

And now she's dead, Iris thought. But her "teammates" probably didn't get much in the way of news here. "What about the other group? Do you ever mix with them?"

"Not since the first day," Hildi said. "Why do you ask?"

She glanced toward Grinkov. He seemed preoccupied by the papers he was shuffling through. She lowered her voice. "The medium is a friend of mine. Maybe you met her—Sandrine Beck?"

The other three exchanged looks. Hildi shrugged. "We barely had time to exchange hellos before Dr. Grinkov split us up into two groups. I think they don't want us mingling— something about maintaining the integrity of the study."

Bailey gestured toward Iris's water bottle. "Drink while you can. They take everything away when the session starts."

Iris opened the bottle and made herself drink, hoping it might settle her rumbling stomach. She downed the whole bottle while she listened to the others discuss the upcoming experiment. Apparently today, with Iris added to the mix, they were going to try an experiment involving a small power plant located at the edge of the laboratory grounds.

Iris forced herself to focus on the conversation, taking mental notes to share with Quinn's contact person whenever he arrived. But crowding the edge of her mind was her growing concern about Sandrine. Was she okay?

And where, exactly, was she?

MADDOX GRABBED the roll of plastic trash bags the maintenance crew foreman handed him and rolled out of the back of the Subaru pickup behind the others, falling into line at the lab's back entrance. He had been assigned to the east wing of the building, along with a merry-faced Dutchman named Piet, who'd been there before and seemed happy to take the lead.

In his clipped, accented English, Piet kept up a running commentary about which rooms they could enter and which rooms were off-limits. If he was curious about what lay hidden behind the doors of the forbidden rooms, he showed no sign of it.

"What's that?" Maddox asked as they started past a room with a glass window set into the door. Pale green curtains covered the window from the inside.

"That is the—what is the word? Sick room?"

"Infirmary?"

"Ya, infirmary." Piet kept going.

Maddox stayed where he was. "They don't have any trash for us to pick up?"

"It is one of the rooms we do not enter," Piet said. "If there were rubbish, it would be waiting out here for us."

Maddox frowned. "Maybe they just forgot to put their trash out today. Shouldn't we at least check? It can't be good for an infirmary to have a bunch of garbage sitting around." Maddox reached for the door handle.

"Wait, you cannot—" Piet started, but Maddox had already opened the door and stepped inside.

The infirmary was a small room with only six beds visible. It looked like an emergency room, with retractable curtains set up in an oval around each bed to afford privacy. Only one bed was occupied. A woman with sandy blond hair lay pale and still against the light green sheets on the bed. An IV drip hung from a portable bedside monitor charting the patient's vital signs. Maddox didn't see anyone else in the room, though a door near the back was marked Authorized Personnel Only.

"You cannot be in here!" Piet tugged at Maddox's sleeve.

"Look, there's a full garbage can." Maddox ignored Piet's anxious tugging and crossed to the occupied bed. He bent to retrieve the plastic garbage sack, taking the opportunity to get a good look at the woman in the bed. His heart squeezed.

It was Iris's missing friend, Sandrine.

Chapter Seventeen

The monitor by Sandrine Beck's bed beeped steadily, red numbers showing heart rate, oxygen saturation and blood pressure. Maddox was no doctor, but from what he could tell, her vitals were in the normal range.

Was she just sleeping? Or was she unconscious?

"We should not be in here!" Piet grabbed Maddox's arm.

Maddox looked over his shoulder at the other man. "What do you suppose is wrong with her?"

"If you stay here much longer, you will have a chance to ask the doctor himself." Piet grimaced. "Come, before we both lose our jobs."

Maddox reluctantly followed Piet out of the infirmary, slipping through the door even as he heard the latch engage on the door at the back of the sick bay. He glanced back through the narrow space between the curtains on the infirmary door and spotted a white-clad female—a nurse?—approach Sandrine's bed.

He turned to look at Piet. "Why don't we split up? It'll speed up the process."

"I am supposed to stay with you and train you."

"How much training does it take to empty a trash can? You take the rest of this section and I'll go on around the corner and work my way back up from there. We make it back out to the truck first and the boss man loves us. Maybe he'll even toss us a few extra bucks for the effort. What do you say?"

Piet frowned as he considered Maddox's proposal. He finally nodded. "We will meet at the end of the hall."

Maddox nodded. "Sure thing."

Not that he had any intention of meeting back up with Piet. He had to warn Iris about the second murder and coax her out of this place before she was the next victim.

"A LITTLE HELP here!" Tom Stanton grated. Sweat beaded his broad forehead and the veins in his neck bulged.

Iris tightened her grip on Tom's arm, trying to clear her mind of everything but the feel of Tom's sweat-dampened skin beneath her fingers. She listened to the sound of his breathing and concentrated on matching her pulse to his.

Suddenly, energy began to build in her fingertips and spread up her arm. It sizzled through her bloodstream, blooming in her chest. Her vision dimmed, her head spun, but she tightened her hold on Tom's arm and rode the sensations, more relieved by the return of her gift than pained by the darkness of the energy coursing through her.

"Excellent!" Grinkov laughed with delight. "Release!"

Iris waited until the others released hands before taking her hand from Tom's arm. He slumped forward and laid his head on his arms. While the flutter of sensations coming from him ebbed, a new, erratic buzz of energy stuttered through her.

"Let me show you what you did." Grinkov turned the monitor toward them. A grainy color picture flickered to life, a static shot of an electrical panel.

"That's the power plant," Hildi said. "That's what I saw."

"Indeed," Grinkov said, beaming at her. "Now watch this."

In the middle of a still image, a small red lever suddenly moved from On to Off. Hildi gasped.

Next to Iris, Bailey uttered a soft, "Oo-rah!"

Grinkov ejected the disk and slipped it into a clear jewel case. "I need to take this to the archives to back it up. I will send Halloran to escort you to your rooms to rest for the afternoon session." He left the room, his steps light and fast. The fluttering energy Iris had been feeling began to fade, and she realized it had been coming from Grinkov.

"Escort us to our rooms?" Iris asked as his words sank in.

"We don't go anywhere without an escort." Bailey frowned.

"An afternoon session?" Tom lifted his head from the table. Dark circles shadowed his bloodshot eyes. Iris felt his pain like a headache throbbing between her temples. She moved closer and laid her hand on his arm, drawing his pain into her.

"How do you do that, anyway?" Bailey asked.

"I don't know," Iris admitted.

She felt a sudden rush of anticipation and realized it wasn't coming from herself or anyone inside the room. A second later, the door to the conference room opened behind her and a low, drawling voice asked, "I'm lookin' for the dorms. Can anybody point me in the right direction?"

Iris twisted in her seat, recognizing the voice.

Maddox Heller stood in the doorway, his hand on the doorknob and a grin slashing dimples into his tanned cheeks. His gaze slid past hers, satisfaction glimmering in his eyes.

She rose to her feet. "I can show you."

"We're supposed to wait for Halloran," Hildi said.

Iris shrugged. "Big deal. He was going to take us to our rooms anyway. I'm just getting a head start."

Bailey stood up. "I'll come with."

Iris exchanged another look with Maddox as she and Bailey caught up with him at the door. He held the door politely for them, putting his hand briefly against the small of her back as he followed them out. In that touch, she felt a chaos of emotions, ranging from anxiety to relief.

"Here are the dormitory rooms," Bailey said as they reached the sleeping quarters. "These four rooms." She opened the first door. "Do me a favor and clean mine first? I'd like to take a nap and I don't want to be disturbed later."

Maddox slanted a look at Iris but entered the room with Bailey. Iris surreptitiously showed him four fingers to let him know which room she was in, then went to her own quarters.

Three minutes later, a knock sounded on her door. She felt the now-familiar buzz of electric energy she'd come to recognize as Boris Grinkov. Taking comfort in knowing that Maddox was within shouting distance, she opened the door. "Dr. Grinkov."

"I told you and the others that you were to wait for Halloran to bring you back to your quarters."

She lifted her chin. "Why an escort? Are we prisoners?"

"Of course not," Grinkov said. "But we conduct experiments for private groups who do not wish their business to be known before they're ready to reveal their findings. We take our security and confidentiality seriously." Iris felt a sense of calm steal over her as Grinkov's anxiety ebbed. "I am sorry you think our guidelines restrictive."

"No," she said with a smile. "I understand. I'll behave."

Grinkov smiled at her choice of words. "Halloran will be by later to escort you and the others to the cafeteria. Cook is preparing seared tuna steaks today. I'm sure you will find them delicious." He gave a curt nod and left the room.

Iris slumped on the edge of the bed, her head still throbbing from the residue of Tom Stanton's distress and her own moment of tension with Grinkov. How was she ever going to find Sandrine if her every move was controlled and choreographed?

She felt a sudden flood of warmth, laced with liberal bits of pure adrenaline, a second before the door opened and Maddox slipped inside. She jumped from the bed and met him halfway, wrapping her arms tightly around his waist and pressing her face against the front of his gray coveralls.

He stroked her hair. "Well, hello to you, too, sugar."

"What are you doing here?"

"Gettin' you out."

"I can't leave. I haven't found Sandrine yet."

He grinned at her, triumph in his eyes. "But I have."

She grabbed his arms. "Where?"

"In the infirmary."

Her heart dropped. "What's wrong with her?"

"I don't know," he admitted. "She's unconscious but her vitals look stable, and she's breathing on her own."

She bit back her panic. "We have to get her out of here."

"And we're gonna do that, sugar, but I have to tell you something first." The sensations coming from him darkened. "Another body washed up. Amanda Marquez."

"The other empath on the list?" Iris's knees wobbled. She found the edge of her bed and sat.

Maddox sat beside her. "You didn't feel my knee this morning, did you? Something's happened to your... whatever it is."

"It's back," she said, surprised by the deluge of relief that flowed from him at her words. "I think it was a temporary thing caused by...overexertion." She darted a look at him.

He arched one eyebrow. "Yeah?"

She flushed and forced her mind away from her memories of the previous night's pleasures. "I've got to get to Sandrine."

"I can show you where the infirmary is. But there are cameras all along the hallways. We'll never escape notice."

"How'd you get here unnoticed?"

"I'm on the cleaning crew. We're crawling all over this place. I'm practically invisible."

"Then we need to shut down the surveillance."

"I'd be happy to go all *Mission: Impossible* for you, maybe swoop down from the ceiling and knock out the security to this place, but I don't have time to set things up."

"Do you know where the security center is?"

He arched an eyebrow. "Yeah, Quinn gave me a schematic."

"That may be all we need." She reached up and gave him a quick kiss on his cheek. "Wait here."

She headed for the door.

IRIS RETURNED to her room five minutes later with three other people, a man and two women. The tallest of the women, a raw-boned redhead, stopped in the doorway, her hands on her hips, and asked, "What the hell is going on here?"

Iris closed the door carefully behind them. "Bailey, this is Maddox Heller. He's not really a cleaning guy. Maddox, this is Bailey, Hildi and Tom. They're in my test group."

Maddox stood and nodded toward the others. "What the hell *is* going on here, Iris?"

"We need to disable security, right? And you know where the security center is located, you said."

He nodded warily. "But—"

"Show us the schematic."

"Oh, my God, you want us to shut down security," Bailey said, moving farther into the room. Her eyes lit up. "Well, it's about damned time! This place is a freakin' prison!"

Maddox looked at Iris, the hair on the back of his neck prickling. Who were these people, really? How did she know they could be trusted? Iris met his gaze with calm assurance, her eyes asking him to trust her. He forced himself to relax.

"Maddox Heller," the man named Tom said suddenly. "You're that Marine, the one in Kaziristan."

Maddox felt Iris's eyes on him, but he didn't look away from Tom's narrowed gaze. "I was."

Tom's face creased with a sudden smile. "Was, hell. Once a Marine, always a Marine, man. Second Battalion, Second Marines myself. Saw time in Haiti. Semper fi."

Maddox couldn't help but return the grin. "Semper fi."

"Heard you got the shaft, man. That's rough. So this place—I take it it's not on the up-and-up?"

Maddox glanced at Iris, who was gazing at him with so much pride it made his head spin. He looked back at Tom. "I think it's a cover for something very dangerous. And I think it just may take all of us to get out of here safely."

Unfolding the schematic, he showed Hildi the location of the security center, while Iris caught them up on what they knew about Boris Grinkov, Tahir Mahmoud and the Telaraña laboratory.

"I SEE IT," Hildi said suddenly, her voice rising with excitement. "It's a black cord, plugged into a panel at the back. Not detachable. It'll have to be ripped out."

Bailey closed her eyes a moment. "I see it, too!" She looked up, a huge grin on her face.

Iris gripped Tom's arm more tightly as his breathing started to speed up and grow a little ragged. Pain hammered into her skull but she held on.

"Let me give it a try." Bailey closed her eyes again.

A sharp, blinding pain slammed into Iris's head. Her grip on Tom's arm started to loosen.

"Don't let go!" he barked at her.

She squeezed her eyes shut against the onslaught of agony and clutched his arm. She felt arms wrap around her from behind, holding her upright. *Maddox.* Warmth stole over her, built a wall between her and the pain, providing blessed relief.

"Got it!" Bailey and Hildi cried at the same moment.

Tom let go of the women, and Iris let go of Tom's arm,

slumping back against Maddox's chest. He stroked her hair back from her forehead and pressed a quick kiss against her temple.

"We have about ten minutes, best guess, before they figure out what's up and either find a backup for the system or call for a security crackdown. Tom, you take this." Maddox pulled a compact 9 mm semiautomatic from an ankle holster. "Fifteen rounds, one in the chamber. Make it count."

Tom took the weapon and gave a firm nod.

"Get the women out through this side entrance to that hiding spot I told you about." Maddox showed Tom the building schematic.

"I'm going with you, Maddox," Iris protested.

He touched her shoulder. "I have to do this one alone, baby. Go with Tom. I'll bring Sandrine out to you and you can do your magic once we're safe. I promise."

Tom opened the door and scanned the hallway. "All clear."

"Go on, Iris. I'll be out before you know it." Maddox kissed her forehead and slipped into the hallway past Tom.

Tension hummed through Iris's skin as they crept toward the exit Maddox had shown them, the anxiety of her companions mingling with her own. They found the exit and started to head outside when Iris felt something slam into her, as strong and tangible as a body blow. She staggered into the wall.

Tom caught her arm. "What is it?"

"I don't know," she admitted. Energy coursed through her, unbridled and fierce. She leaned against the wall, trying to catch her breath. "Something strong—out of control—"

"Oh, my God," Hildi breathed. Her gaze was distant and her face had gone pale. "The building…"

A new pulse wave shot through Iris. A familiar tingling sensation set in, like her limbs were going numb.

Grinkov.

But this sensation was stronger than she'd felt from him before, and much more unbridled.

"We have to get out of here," Hildi said with a gasp. "The support columns are starting to buckle. I see cracks forming—"

"I have to warn Maddox!" As Iris pushed away from the wall, a faint tremor made the world tilt under her feet.

For a moment she thought it was more of the same sensations she'd been feeling, but she heard Bailey utter a low profanity and growl, "Earthquake?"

The building was giving way, Iris realized. Whatever was happening with Grinkov was threatening the construction integrity of the lab. She turned to Tom. "Get them out of here. I think I know what's causing this. And I have to slow it down until Maddox and Sandrine can get out."

"What are you talking about?" Tom asked.

"Grinkov has latent telekinetic abilities. I've felt it when I'm around him. It's like electricity pushing through me. It's kind of what I feel from Bailey, only with Grinkov, it's unleashed. It's emotion-based, and he can't control it."

"What about the others?" Bailey asked.

Iris wasn't sure there were any others, but she promised to send them out if she ran across anyone. Tom gave her an uncertain look but finally nodded and led Hildi and Bailey out.

Iris closed her eyes a moment, trying to get a direction on the energy slamming its way down the laboratory corridors. It seemed to be focused in the direction from which she and the others had just come.

She took a bracing breath and headed down the hallway.

MADDOX SLIPPED through the infirmary door, weapon drawn, and quickly scanned the room. Sandrine Beck was where he'd last seen her, but this time, she wasn't alone. A caramel-skinned nurse with wavy black hair tied in a ponytail low on her neck stood at her bedside, changing the IV bag. She turned at the sound of the door opening.

"You're not authorized to be here—" she began, then stopped quickly as her gaze fell on the Glock in Maddox's hand.

"I believe I am." Maddox stayed alert as he crossed to the bed. "Is there anyone else here?"

"There's someone in the back," the nurse said quickly. Too quickly. Maddox knew a lie when he heard one.

"No, there's not." He glanced at Sandrine's pale, still face. "What's wrong with her?"

"We're not sure," the nurse admitted. "She fell ill after the first session."

"Why didn't you transfer her to the hospital in Sebastian?"

The nurse laughed mirthlessly, eyeing Maddox's weapon. "Believe me, our facilities, staff and equipment are closer to what you'll find in the States than anything the Sebastian hospital can provide. This was the best place for her."

"The best place for her was with people who gave a damn

about her in the first place," Maddox growled. "Can she be unhooked from this stuff? Is any of it life-sustaining?"

The ground under their feet shifted suddenly. Maddox grabbed the cold metal headboard with his free hand to steady himself. It felt like an earthquake. Almost.

"What was that?" The nurse's eyes widened.

Nearby, a ceiling tile fell to the floor with a loud smack. The nurse whirled around at the sound.

A low vibration buzzed through the floor beneath Maddox's feet, feeding his urgency. "Can we unhook her and get her out of here?" he asked the nurse.

"You want us to wheel her out of here on a gurney? To where?" The nurse found her backbone suddenly, apparently alarmed at the thought of hauling her patient around.

Maddox found her concern encouraging. "Something's happening here. I don't think this building is safe."

The nurse eyed the gun. "What do you want me to do?"

"Can we strap her in a wheelchair instead of a gurney?"

The nurse gave him a worried look, but she nodded and headed into the back room to retrieve a chair.

As they headed down the hallway, the nurse pushing the chair and Maddox bringing up the rear, the vibrations rumbling beneath his feet grew stronger. Along the walls of the building, Sheetrock buckled and threw off chunks that littered the tile floors underfoot. Maddox pushed the nurse to move faster, building their pace to a slow jog as they navigated through the falling debris toward the side exit.

They ran across several alarmed members of the cleaning crew, but oddly, no security guards. Maddox directed the cleaning crew to the exit. One of the men held the door for the nurse and Sandrine while Maddox kept an eye out for security teams. He heard a crashing noise from somewhere behind them, but there was no sign of any pursuers.

He followed the others into the sheeting rain, shrugging out of his coveralls to make a makeshift umbrella for Sandrine. He'd given Tom directions to a place to hide the others until he arrived. It was slow going for the wheelchair, the wheels sinking into the rain-soaked ground underfoot. But with the help of Piet and the other maintenance crew, they made it before the rain soaked through the coveralls.

"Thank God you're here!" Tom greeted him with a smile and hearty handshake. He waved the plastic-covered satellite phone at Maddox. "The cavalry should be here in fifteen minutes."

"Where's Iris?" Maddox asked.

Tom looked surprised. "I thought she'd be with you."

Maddox's stomach knotted. "What?"

"She went back in to warn you about what was happening. She thought she knew what was causing it, and she said she could hold it back long enough for you and her friend to get out safely. You didn't run into her?"

Before Maddox could answer, a muted crack came from the direction of the laboratory, so faint that most of the others seemed not to notice. But Maddox did. So did Tom. They exchanged looks of alarm.

It had been a gunshot.

Chapter Eighteen

The ground shuddered under Iris's feet, and she staggered against the wall. She had told the others that Grinkov was telekinetic, but now she wasn't sure she was right. Whatever was happening here, she couldn't imagine Grinkov was doing it on purpose, for along with the sparking of energy came rolling waves of unadulterated panic. Grinkov was terrified, and that fear was finding substance through the energy pulsing through the laboratory, leaving chaos in its wake.

The combination of sensations overwhelmed her, driving her to her knees. She twisted until she was sitting with her back to the wall, trying to absorb the shock waves of Grinkov's unfettered energy, hoping it would be enough to keep the lab from falling down around them before they could safely escape.

But the waves kept coming, rising on an angry sea of emotion. A large chunk of ceiling crashed into the floor a few feet from Iris, shattering into dozens of pieces that skittered across the tile floor, dusting her with fine shards of Sheetrock. She blinked as particles stung her eyes and tried to push to her feet.

Suddenly, blinding pain exploded behind her eyes, and the world went black for a moment. It took a second for Iris to realize that the ringing sound in her ears was the dying echo of a gunshot ringing through the laboratory's maze of hallways.

The flood of energy was gone.

Her vision seeped back, bringing with it the dim lights lining the corridors. Though the surge of energy had abated, debris continued to fall in sporadic thuds around her, echoing down the hallways.

She no longer felt anything from Boris Grinkov, not even pain. Only a cavernous emptiness she'd never felt before, not even from Alexander Quinn.

Grinkov was dead, she realized, her stomach twisting.

The nausea built, thick and fetid. She swallowed convulsively, pushing herself up the wall into a standing position. Sudden, dark emotions shook her, pushing her back to the floor. Rage. Hate. Vicious determination.

Footsteps moved closer, coming down the hallway around the corner. The urge to run pushed her back to her feet again, but the only two exits she knew of both lay around the corner. The person she heard approaching stood between her and escape.

She started to run in the other direction, but her legs wouldn't move. Her knees buckling, she fell to the floor, catching herself with her hands. Pieces of Sheetrock dug into her palms, but she barely felt the sting, too overwhelmed by the approaching darkness. A hard pain formed in her side, as if someone had kicked her. She found it difficult to breathe.

She pushed to her feet again and leaned against the wall, turning her head toward the sound of the approaching footsteps. Through tears of pain, she saw it was a man dressed in black jeans and a black long-sleeved shirt. A black ski mask covered his face, but as he strode purposefully toward her, his steps slow and steady, she glimpsed a pale patch of skin on the inside of his left wrist.

Tahir Mahmoud, she realized with a sinking heart.

"THAT WAS a gunshot, wasn't it?" Tom asked.

Maddox double-checked the Glock's 18-round clip and tried to hide his rising panic. "Yeah. I'm going back in to get Iris."

"I'll go with you."

Maddox shook his head. "Someone has to protect these people until the extraction team arrives."

"Be careful," Tom said.

Swallowing a wave of nausea, Maddox nodded and headed back toward the lab.

Maddox stepped inside, took a deep breath, and listened over the thunder of his pulse. The building was unnaturally quiet; from their hiding place, they'd seen several vehicles speeding away from the laboratory, while other people ran down the rutted roads through the driving rain. Was anyone besides Iris left inside?

He took a few steps down the hallway, wincing as his toe caught a chunk of ceiling and sent it clattering down the hallway in front of him. The hallway was dim, lit only by low-wattage emergency lights. Apparently whatever had caused the building to shake had knocked out the power, as well.

He crept down the hall, taking care not to displace any more debris, and turned the corner. Ahead in the gloom, he spotted what looked like a body lying in a heap halfway down the hall. Panic overcame caution for a moment, and he raced toward the crumpled form.

Halfway there, he realized that it was a man's body. The man lay facedown, drenched in blood from what could only be a gunshot wound to the head. There was no way to be sure, but it was the right build for the Russian scientist, Grinkov.

He skirted the body, avoiding the blood spreading across the tiles at his feet. Someone else hadn't been as careful, he noted, spotting bloodstained footprints heading down the hall.

Tightening his grip on the Glock, he followed the footprints as they turned the corner to another corridor.

And stopped dead.

Fifteen feet away, a man dressed in black from head to foot stood with a gun to Iris's head.

Maddox whipped into firing stance on instinct.

"Do not do it, Sergeant." Tahir Mahmoud's clipped British accent was unmistakable. "I will kill her. You know that."

Maddox felt his vision blacken at the edges. He fought the gut-churning déjà vu and met Iris's terrified gaze.

Not this time, he thought, taking slow breaths to steady himself. *I won't let it happen this time.*

"I SEE YOU FIND THIS as familiar as I." Tahir Mahmoud's breath burned against Iris's ear. He pushed the barrel of his weapon into her temple. "I would have liked to use a knife to make it truly authentic, but one does what one must."

"You know who I am," Maddox said.

"Of course. I know everything about you. When associates told me about Grinkov's experiments here on Mariposa, I knew I had to come here myself."

"Because I was here," Maddox murmured.

"I've been thinking about this a long time, you know. You cheated last time. Let a woman spill her blood to save you."

Maddox's face blanched as his gaze shifted from Tahir's face to lock with Iris's. She felt his fear, his pain, his shame, but she also felt something she'd never really sensed from him before. Pride. Determination. And a growing strength of will pouring into her veins like liquid fire.

"Put down the gun, Heller."

Maddox hesitated. Tahir knocked the gun barrel against the side of Iris's head. She tried to bite back a cry of pain.

"Do it now," Tahir ordered.

"You're going to kill her anyway, aren't you?" Maddox asked, not budging. "This is your game. You kill her in front of me. Then you kill me like you didn't get to do last time."

Tahir laughed. Pain shot through Iris's side, making her gasp. He was injured, she realized. Maybe a cracked rib.

"I'm not playing your game, Tahir."

"You have no choice." Tahir dropped the gun to Iris's belly. "I can shoot her now. Gut shot. It won't kill her right away. She'll just wish she were dead. You can make it hard for her. Or you can make it easy."

"Don't do it!" Iris said.

But Maddox bent and laid his gun on the floor at his feet.

"There's no honor in killing a woman who has done nothing to you. How does that promote your jihad?"

"Jihad?" Tahir laughed in Iris's ear. "Do you believe everything your television tells you? This is not about religion. This is about power. My country is up for grabs, Sergeant. My very oil-rich country. Only the daring will rule."

"And killing an unarmed woman is daring?"

"It will give me a story to tell to those whom I wish to influence," Tahir said. "Now kick the gun over here."

Maddox pushed the gun across the floor with his foot.

Tahir began to lift the gun back to Iris's head, giving her the opening she'd hoped for. She whipped her elbow back into Tahir's injured rib cage, grunting as she heard a snapping sound. She pitched forward, swallowed by agony, slipping from Tahir's loosened grasp. Her vision darkened as something rushed past her. Maddox, she realized, diving for Tahir.

Biting back pain, she scrambled for Maddox's gun a few feet away. Nearby, Maddox and Tahir struggled over Tahir's weapon, the Kaziristani putting up a vicious fight despite his injury. Maddox jerked the ski mask from the man's head and stared at him a moment, as if to assure himself he had the right man. Then he slammed Tahir's hand against the wall, knocking the gun loose. It clattered to the floor and slid down the hall away from them.

A shuddering rumble built underneath Iris's knees as she grabbed for Maddox's gun. The whole building began to shake, huge chunks of ceiling and wall starting to fall around them.

Tahir slammed his head against Maddox's, knocking him backward. Maddox lost his grip on the Kaziristani, who turned and started running down the hall.

Maddox started to give chase, but an enormous chunk

of the ceiling fell in his path, showering him with debris. A cracking sound drew Iris's eyes upward, and she saw a support beam sagging precariously through the gap in the ceiling. "Maddox!" she cried as the beam started to come unmoored. "Let him go! The place is going to collapse!"

He looked up as the beam snapped free and started to fall. Scrambling out of the way, he grabbed Tahir's discarded gun, tucked it in the waistband of his jeans and raced to Iris. Taking his own weapon from her shaking hands, he half pushed, half carried her toward the exit at the end of the hallway.

They burst into the rain-washed air outside as the rumbling behind them grew to deafening proportions. An explosion rocked the jungle, the shock wave slamming into their backs. Maddox grabbed Iris as she lost her footing. He lifted her over his shoulder and carried her fireman-style into the jungle.

Tom Stanton greeted them as they reached the rendezvous point, his gaze moving toward the laboratory. Maddox looked behind him and saw that the building had begun a slow, thunderous implosion, the outer walls toppling in on themselves.

He set Iris on her feet. She sagged against him, agony etched in her delicate features. "There are people in there—"

Maddox caught her face between his hands. "Look at me."

She struggled to focus her gaze on his face.

"Give it to me, Iris. Let go of it and give it to me."

She seemed uncertain what he was asking for a moment, but he bent his forehead to hers and whispered. "Give it to me."

He saw understanding in her eyes just before they fluttered closed. He couldn't feel whatever she was releasing into him through her touch, but her cheeks grew pink and the tension in her body melted away. Her knees buckled and he caught her up in his arms, pressing a kiss to her temple. "There you go."

She lifted her head. "Sandrine?"

"Right over here, baby." He helped her to the wheelchair where a camouflage-clad man was checking Sandrine's vitals.

"Sandrine!" she cried, grabbing her friend's arm. She swayed slightly, and Maddox eased her to a crouch by the wheelchair, tucking himself behind her to cradle her body while she talked to her friend. He felt her trembling and tightened his grip, pressing a soft kiss to her temple.

Sandrine's eyes fluttered open. "Iris?"

"That's right, Sandy. It's me. I found you."

Sandrine managed a weak smile. "I knew you would."

The medic gently removed Iris's hand from Sandrine's arm, slanting a look at Maddox. Maddox returned the gaze, daring the man to say a word.

He kissed Iris's hair. "Let's get out of here, baby."

As soon as the extraction team delivered the survivors to the U.S. consulate, Quinn and a pair of grim-looking CIA types had separated everyone out for questioning. Now, twenty-four hours later, Maddox had reached the end of his patience.

He knew now why Sandrine Beck had been spared—apparently Grinkov and Mahmoud had ordered tests to determine how the experiments had caused her coma in the hopes of counteracting those side effects in the future. He knew that Mahmoud had ordered lab security to dispose of Celia Shore and Andrea Marquez once Grinkov determined they were faking their so-called psychic abilities.

What he didn't know was where the hell Iris was and why they wouldn't let him see her.

"I want out of here," he growled at the interrogator across the table from him. "I've answered every damn question three times, and nothing has changed. Where's Quinn? I want to talk to Alexander Quinn."

A moment later, verifying Maddox's certainty that he was being observed, Quinn entered the cramped interrogation room. "What do you want?"

Maddox rose to his feet. "Out."

"We have more questions—"

"That's crap and you know it. Where is Iris Browning?"

Quinn glanced at his watch. "Probably boarding a plane to the States as we speak."

"What?" Maddox's heart dropped. She'd left? No good-bye, no "Thanks, it's been fun"? Pain settled in his chest, black and hot.

"Now, can we get back to the questions?" Quinn asked.

"How about you answering one for me?" He closed the distance between himself and Quinn, letting his gathering pain feed his anger. "Did you find Mahmoud?"

"Yes. We found Grinkov, as well. Both dead."

He thought he'd feel relief. He didn't. "What about the experiments?"

Quinn shook his head. "We debriefed the participants. There are any number of uses for the sort of infiltration

Grinkov and the focus-group members were experimenting with."

And now the CIA knew what Iris and her friends could do. Was that why Quinn was keeping him away from Iris? "Can I go now?"

"We have a few more questions—"

"No, you don't," Nicholas Darcy said from the doorway. "Mr. Heller, thank you for your cooperation. I will be happy to return you to your home now." The RSO glared at Quinn as if daring him to argue.

Quinn gave a shrug and got out of the way.

"Thanks, man. I owe you," Maddox told Darcy as they walked through the back hallway of the consulate building.

"Quinn is an ass." Darcy opened a door and bright sunlight slanted through the opening, making Maddox squint. He followed Darcy into the consulate's back lot, where a dark sedan was idling. Darcy turned to look at him. "The plane to the U.S. is currently waiting out a twenty-minute boarding delay. I've instructed the driver to take you to the airport posthaste."

Maddox stared at the RSO, a flutter of hope tickling his chest. "You're a stand-up guy, Darcy."

Darcy's lips twitched, but he managed to hold back a smile. "I wouldn't delay if I were you."

Maddox settled in the backseat of the sedan, his heart pounding with a mixture of anticipation and anxiety.

Iris paced the boarding gate area, glaring at the CIA agent keeping watch a few feet away. Sandrine sat in a wheelchair nearby, watching her with a bemused expression.

"Wearing a hole in the carpet won't make them let us board any faster."

Iris pressed her lips into a thin line. She didn't want to board any faster. She didn't want to board at all.

Not without seeing Maddox one last time. Not without knowing if he shared the ripping sensation currently burning through her gut at the thought of never seeing him again.

Sandrine caught her hand, stilling her movements. "You don't want to go, do you?"

Iris slumped into a nearby chair. "Why are they rushing us out of here? You're not even recovered yet." She and Sandrine had spent the night St. Ignacio Hospital, and while Sandrine had improved drastically, Iris had been surprised when Alexander Quinn had arrived that morning and told them they were booked on a 10 a.m. flight to the U.S.

She'd asked about Maddox. Quinn claimed not to know where he was and suggested she try phoning him on the way to the airport. But so far, Maddox hadn't answered her calls.

What if he didn't want to see her again, now that the mystery of Sandrine's disappearance had been solved? What if all she'd ever been to him was a diversion to pass the time?

The sound of a scuffle elsewhere in the terminal drew her attention. Frustration tinged with anxiety slammed into her as she recognized Maddox's voice. "You damn well are going to let me through!"

She jumped up and raced toward the cluster of guards she saw gathered about twenty yards away, catching the CIA guard by surprise. Maddox was grappling with two uniformed security guards at the security gate, but he looked up as she called his name. His blue eyes lit up from the inside, and the sensation that washed through her made her knees wobble and her heart sing. "Iris!"

She tried to pull the guards away from him. "Let him go!"

A Sebastian policeman entered the fray, speaking quietly to the security guards. A moment later, they let Maddox go, and he pushed through the guards to grab Iris in a bear hug.

"I thought I wasn't going to make it in time," he murmured in her ear.

"So did I," she admitted, burying her face in his neck.

He let go and cradled her cheeks between his hands, searching her face. "Are you okay?"

"I'm fine." She tucked a lock of overlong hair behind his ear. "How about you? You look tired."

His expression relaxed, dimples forming as he managed a smile. "You know Quinn—loves to whip out the thumbscrews."

She scowled. "He said he didn't know where you were."

"Baby, you're surprised that Superspook lied to you?"

"I'm glad you're here."

Behind them, Sandrine cleared her throat. "You must be Maddox. We didn't get a proper introduction the other day during the whatever you call it."

"Extraction," Iris supplied.

"Nice to meet you, finally," Maddox said.

Behind her, the CIA agent shot Maddox a dark look and cleared his throat. "The plane is boarding." He grabbed the handles of Sandrine's wheelchair.

"Wait just a minute," Iris said. "I'm not through here."

"Your plane is leaving in ten minutes. If you don't get a move on now—"

"Give us a minute," Iris said sharply.

The agent frowned but pushed Sandrine's wheelchair toward the loading gate, leaving them alone.

Iris turned to look at Maddox. His slate-blue eyes were slightly narrowed as he returned her gaze. "Do you want me to go?" she asked softly.

He threaded his fingers through her hair. "No. I want you here with me."

"Why?" she asked, although she could already feel the reason why, sweeping through her in joyous waves.

He managed a watery smile. "Because I love you."

"I love you, too," she whispered against his lips before she kissed him.

He deepened the kiss, staking claim to her with a hunger that left her shaken.

She reluctantly withdrew. "I have to go with Sandrine. I can't abandon her now."

"I know." He kissed her. "You know where to find me."

A minor chord drifted into the symphony of happiness soaring through her. Coming from Maddox.

It was homesickness, she realized with a start.

She brushed her lips over his again. "Or you could come with me. There's another flight in an hour. We could change our tickets, buy you one, and all go back together."

The minor key darkened with a combination of longing and dread. "I can't go back."

"But you want to."

The desire in his eyes was unmistakable.

"You won't be alone in this," she said. "There are a lot of people who believe in you back home."

He cupped her cheek. "All I care about is what you think."

"I think you should come home with me. I want you to meet my sisters and their husbands. I have a beautiful niece and a nephew on the way. We'll be your family."

"Do you have any idea what you're getting yourself into?"

She kissed him again. "Do you?"

He laughed, hugging her tight. And for the first time in a long, long time, Iris felt nothing but pure, soaring joy.

Epilogue

Five months later

"Naughty man!" Iris's breath was hot in Maddox's ear as he hustled toward the bride's room.

"Isn't that why you married me, sugar?" He nuzzled the nape of her neck. She made a low moaning sound that shot straight to his groin.

"What if someone comes looking for us?" As they reached the bride's room door, she turned in his arms and lifted her face to him. He pushed her back against the door and kissed her hard and deep. She wound her arms around his neck and pulled him closer, matching his passion with fire of her own.

He reached around her, fumbling for the doorknob. His hand closed around the cool metal and gave it a quick twist, clutching her waist to keep from falling inside the room as the door swung open.

She pulled him into the room with her, her tongue warm and urgent against his.

"I see congratulations are in order."

Iris stumbled, clutching Maddox to keep from falling. They broke away from each other and turned to look at the man lounging on a dainty bench in front of the bride's vanity on the far side of the room.

"Quinn," Maddox growled, not believing his eyes.

"I realize it's customary to bring a gift." Alexander Quinn rose, his movements controlled and unhurried. "I suppose I've done that, though I'm not sure you'll like it."

Iris glanced at Maddox, no doubt gauging his emotions to see if she should intervene. He tamped down his growing irritation and released a long sigh. "You obviously came here to tell us something. So get on with it. We've got a honeymoon to start."

"Al-Adar is out to avenge Mahmoud's death."

Maddox felt his blood go cold. "What?"

He felt Iris's hand on his arm. He closed his hand over hers, grateful for her calming touch.

"You could have just called with that information," Iris said to Quinn. "What else do you want from us?"

Quinn smiled at Iris, the expression as close to genuine as Maddox had ever seen from the CIA agent. "You look beautiful, Mrs. Heller. Best wishes for a long and happy life." His gaze hardened as he turned it toward Maddox. "To both of you."

"Meaning?"

"You're a wealthy man, Heller. That's a plus when you have a target on your back." Quinn moved slowly past them toward the door before turning to look back at them. "The government can't protect individuals. Not efficiently. And there are jobs they can't—or won't—do. It occurs to me that this world could use people who can—and will—do those jobs."

He left the room, closing the door behind him.

Iris looked up at Maddox, her grip tightening on his arm. "He's right. The world could use people like that."

Maddox closed his fingers over hers, more aware than ever before just how much he loved her.

"I know," he said.

"So what are you going to do?" she asked.

"You in the mood to save the world, baby?" he asked.

A smile curved her lips. "I thought you'd never ask."

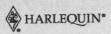

REQUEST YOUR FREE BOOKS!

2 FREE NOVELS PLUS 2 FREE GIFTS!

✦ HARLEQUIN®
INTRIGUE®

Breathtaking Romantic Suspense

YES! Please send me 2 FREE Harlequin Intrigue® novels and my 2 FREE gifts. After receiving them, if I don't wish to receive any more books, I can return the shipping statement marked "cancel." If I don't cancel, I will receive 6 brand-new novels every month and be billed just $4.24 per book in the U.S., or $4.99 per book in Canada, plus 25¢ shipping and handling per book and applicable taxes, if any*. That's a savings of close to 15% off the cover price! I understand that accepting the 2 free books and gifts places me under no obligation to buy anything. I can always return a shipment and cancel at any time. Even if I never buy another book from Harlequin, the two free books and gifts are mine to keep forever.

182 HDN EEZ7   382 HDN EEZK

Name	(PLEASE PRINT)	
Address		Apt. #
City	State/Prov.	Zip/Postal Code

Signature (if under 18, a parent or guardian must sign)

Mail to the **Harlequin Reader Service®**:
IN U.S.A.: P.O. Box 1867, Buffalo, NY 14240-1867
IN CANADA: P.O. Box 609, Fort Erie, Ontario L2A 5X3

Not valid to current Harlequin Intrigue subscribers.

Want to try two free books from another line?
Call 1-800-873-8635 or visit www.morefreebooks.com.

* Terms and prices subject to change without notice. NY residents add applicable sales tax. Canadian residents will be charged applicable provincial taxes and GST. This offer is limited to one order per household. All orders subject to approval. Credit or debit balances in a customer's account(s) may be offset by any other outstanding balance owed by or to the customer. Please allow 4 to 6 weeks for delivery.

Your Privacy: Harlequin is committed to protecting your privacy. Our Privacy Policy is available online at www.eHarlequin.com or upon request from the Reader Service. From time to time we make our lists of customers available to reputable firms who may have a product or service of interest to you. If you would prefer we not share your name and address, please check here. ☐

HI07

**Don't miss
the latest thriller from**

AMANDA
STEVENS

On sale March 2008!

 off the purchase price of
**THE DEVIL'S FOOTPRINTS
by Amanda Stevens.**

Offer valid from March 1, 2008 to May 31, 2008. Redeemable at
participating retail outlets. Limit one coupon per purchase.

52608155

5 65373 00076 2 (8100) 0 11460

MAS2530CPN

HARLEQUIN®
Super Romance®

Bundles of Joy—
coming next month to Superromance

Experience the romance, excitement and joy with 6 heartwarming titles.

BABY, I'M YOURS #1476 by *Carrie Weaver*

ANOTHER MAN'S BABY
(The Tulanes of Tennessee)
#1477 by *Kay Stockham*

THE MARINE'S BABY (9 Months Later)
#1478 by *Rogenna Brewer*

BE MY BABIES (Twins)
#1479 by *Kathryn Shay*

THE DIAPER DIARIES (Suddenly a Parent)
#1480 by *Abby Gaines*

HAVING JUSTIN'S BABY (A Little Secret)
#1481 by *Pamela Bauer*

Exciting, Emotional and Unexpected!

Look for these Superromance titles in March 2008.
Available wherever books are sold.

HARLEQUIN® *Romance*®

MEDITERRANEAN DADS

In the first of this emotional Mediterranean Dads duet, nanny Julie is whisked away to a palatial Italian villa, but she feels completely out of place in Massimo's glamorous world. Her biggest challenge, though, is ignoring her attraction to the brooding tycoon.

Look for

The Italian Tycoon and the Nanny

by **Rebecca** Winters

in March wherever you buy books.

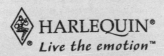

HARLEQUIN®
Live the emotion™

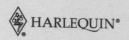

INTRIGUE®

COMING NEXT MONTH

#1047 IN NAME ONLY? by Patricia Rosemoor
The McKenna Legacy
This wasn't Michael Eagan's first high-profile murder case—but it *was* his first McKenna. He'll have to be a good man to charm Flanna, and live dangerously to keep her alive.

#1048 MYSTERIOUS MILLIONAIRE by Cassie Miles
Wealthy adventurer Dylan Crawford is a man of many secrets. So when Elle Norton goes undercover on his estate to investigate a family death, what she discovers about the man is more revealing than she expected.

#1049 WYOMING MANHUNT by Ann Voss Peterson
Thriller
Riding horseback through the Wyoming wilderness was supposed to be the trip of a lifetime for Shanna Clarke—instead she found herself running for her life. Now only rancher Jace Lantry can help her find justice—and exact revenge.

#1050 THE HORSEMAN'S SON by Delores Fossen
Five-Alarm Babies
Collena Drake thought she'd never see her son again after he was stolen at birth. But she found him, in the care of Dylan Greer, a wealthy Texas horse breeder with a dark past. Despite their differences, the two would have to work together to uncover an illegal adoption ring to build their new family.

#1051 AVENGING ANGEL by Alice Sharpe
Elle Medina was the sole survivor of a brutal slaying—and sought to bring down the crime boss that set it off. Undercover DEA agent Pete Waters was tasked with keeping that man alive. At cross purposes, neither knew mercy—in love or death.

#1052 TEXAS-SIZED SECRETS by Elle James
Cattle rustlers, ranch foreclosure and pregnancy were all Texas-sized problems that even Mona Grainger wasn't stubborn enough to think she could handle alone. Enter Reed Bryson, who could ride, rope, kiss… and certainly handle a gun.

www.eHarlequin.com